Amy and the Sorrel Summer

Amy and the Sorrel Summer
116117

by Laura H. Fisher

Illustrated by Sheila Greenwald

Holt, Rinehart and Winston

New York · Chicago · San Francisco

92838-0114
Printed in the United States of America
First Edition

for Cari

Chapter 1

Amy Jackson slid down from the rail fence that enclosed the pigpen and picked up her school books. "Berne, let's go now," she said to her brother, who was two years her senior.

"Okay," Berne replied, but he made no move to go. He leaned farther over the fence and stirred his large hand in the cluster of baby pigs that were gathered near. They tumbled together in a mass of grunts and squeals. The sow came running to protect them, swinging her head in a threatening manner and, in her hurry, knocking down more of her babies than Berne had.

Berne laughed.

"Come on, Berne," Amy tried again, as she

glanced toward the mountains where black clouds were spilling into the valley.

"Silly old pig, I won't hurt your babies," Berne chuckled.

"It's going to rain, Berne, and Miss Applegate won't like it if her *Favorite Horses* gets wet." Miss Applegate was Amy's schoolteacher, and she certainly wouldn't have let Amy take home the brand-new book, *Favorite Horse Stories,* if she had known it was going by way of a pigpen and now possibly a rainstorm.

Berne stepped away from the pen and walked down the road at Amy's side. But he was in no hurry. With his blond hair bouncing on his forehead, he sauntered leisurely and whistled "The Old Chisholm Trail." "The Old Chisholm Trail" was Berne's favorite tune, except when he was especially happy; then he whistled "I'm an Old Cowhand from the Rio Grande." Both tunes were very hard to whistle, especially "The Old Chisholm Trail." It jumped around so.

"Mother will be wondering why we are so late coming home from school." Amy walked a little faster.

"Mother won't care that we went over to Sheriff Jensen's barn to see the mud that washed up against it during last night's thunderstorm." Berne stopped and looked back past the pigpen to the door of the cow barn. "That's sure a pile of mud and rocks, just like the kids at school said. The Sheriff will have to get machinery to dig out his doorway before he can milk inside again."

With a few quick strides of his long legs, Berne

caught up with Amy; then walking slowly again he kicked at the gravel, sending pebbles into the weeds.

A few drops of rain touched Amy's cheeks. She carefully tucked *Favorite Horse Stories* between *Peoples Around the World* and *Arithmetic Grade 5*. If they had only gone the four blocks straight home from school instead of this roundabout way by Sheriff Jensen's on the south side of town, they would have been home by now.

Lightning zigzagged through the black clouds hanging over the canyon mouth, and thunder rolled from the canyon, filling the valley with its rumblings. The raindrops quickened on Amy's cheeks.

"Oh, Berne, it's raining," Amy cried.

"Uh-huh," said Berne, and he tilted his face toward the sky, letting the rain fall full on it. Amy tilted her face up also, even opening her mouth a little to better feel the rain's coolness. She loved to be out in the rain. If only it weren't for Miss Applegate's *Favorite Horses* . . . She drew her books closer to her. Another flash of lightning seemed to split the sky open, and the rain began to fall in torrents.

"Come on," shouted Berne. He dashed down the road, slipped between the wires of a gate, and sprinted off along a lane toward a barn that stood back in a field. Clinging tightly to her books and bending over them to shield them from the rain, Amy ducked under the barbed wire of the gate. She ran down the lane as fast as she could and reached the shelter of the barn's overhanging roof not long after Berne.

"It's still dry." Amy peeked cautiously at Miss Applegate's book. She smoothed down her wrinkled skirt and pressed back her wet blonde hair, then stood and looked out at the rain that was rapidly turning the lane into a stream.

"Berne," asked Amy, looking anxiously up and down the road, "is this Mr. Peneck's barn?"

"You know it is," he answered, trying to sound unconcerned. "Let's go in."

He pushed open the small door against which he had been leaning and stepped inside.

"Berne, I don't think we'd better. I mean maybe Mr. Peneck wouldn't like it," Amy worried.

But Berne had disappeared from the doorway. Amy looked carefully in both directions, half expecting to see Mr. Peneck splashing through the rain shaking his fist in front of him. She decided right then to follow Berne, for if Mr. Peneck did come along, it would be much better to be in the barn with her brother than to be outside all alone.

She stepped through the door which Berne had left open and into the dark interior of the barn. When her eyes became accustomed to the darkness, she saw that she was in a small room where the saddles were kept.

"Berne," she called softly, "Berne."

There was no answer. She walked timidly across the room, stopping by a big black-and-white leather saddle.

"Berne," she whispered.

"Boo!" she heard from directly above her. Amy looked up to see Berne's grinning face hanging from a square doorway in the ceiling.

"You just quit that, Berne Arthur Jackson," ordered Amy, much relieved to see him instead of Mr. Peneck.

"Come on up," Berne said, and his head disappeared from the doorway.

Amy moved her books to her left arm so the right one was free for climbing. The ladder which led to the doorway was nailed to the wall. She stepped onto it and pulled herself through the small doorway into the hayloft, which was empty at this time of year because there was plenty of pasture for the animals and the first crop of hay had not yet been put up. Amy walked through the dust of dried leaves, all that was left of last year's hay, to Berne, who sat in front of one of the huge, open doors through which Mr. Peneck would put his new hay in a few weeks.

Amy sat down cross-legged next to Berne and peered out the doorway at the rain, which was still falling in sheets. "I hope Mr. Peneck doesn't mind us being in his barn."

"We had to get out of the rain," stated Berne.

"Yes," Amy worried, "but Mr. Peneck doesn't like kids." Every kid in town knew that. Why it was only last fall that Amy, Berne, and Jill, their five-year-old sister, had seen Mr. Peneck come marching up the road leading Hurley Thick by the ear. Hurley Thick was their neighbor and often did things for which he deserved to be led by the ear, but usually people put up with him without complaining, for Hurley's father had died when he was a little boy and his mother had enough to worry about without the trouble Hurley caused. But Mr. Peneck led Hurley right up the Thick's path and onto the porch, saying all the time in a very loud voice that he had better not catch Hurley riding his calves again.

"Let's read a story," said Berne, taking *Favorite Horse Stories* from Amy's lap. He opened the book in the middle. "This one called 'The Ghost Horse' looks good," he said, peering at a picture of a dark meadow, in the middle of which was the shadowy outline of a horse. Amy thought the story looked good too, so they sat together in the dimly lit hayloft while the rain pelted down outside and Berne read aloud.

The story was about a boy who had moved into a Western town where there were many rumors of a ghost horse that would run about the countryside at night, frightening people and doing strange deeds. It was the ghost of a stallion that had belonged to an Indian chief whose hunting grounds had included the territory where the town now stood.

"A neighbor, Mr. Sawyer, told of the strange noises he heard one night," Berne read. "And how, on looking out the window, he had seen his corral gate torn down and two of his mares following a white figure into the wooded slopes around his farm. The next morn . . ."

THUD! THUD!

"What was that?" Amy whispered, not daring to move.

Berne shook his head.

THUD! THUD! SCRAPE!

"It might be Mr. Peneck," whispered Amy, "or it might be a . . . a . . . a ghost horse." Of all the people she knew, Mr. Peneck would be most likely to have a ghost horse.

THUD! THUD! BUMP!

Berne quietly handed Amy the book. He stood up and walked silently to the far side of the hayloft, where hatches were cut to allow hay to be pushed down to the stalls below.

THUD! THUD!

Berne bent down and cautiously pushed the hinged hatch cover out a couple of inches. He peered through the crack into the dimness below. Suddenly he dropped the cover back into place, sat straight up, threw his head back, and laughed a laugh that filled the whole barn and echoed back and forth among the rafters.

Amy walked over to the hatch, pushed the cover up and looked down into the stalls. "Why, Berne," she exclaimed, "it's a horse—no, it's three horses."

Berne pulled the cover up, hooked it open, and leaned out over the stalls to get a better look. His sister crowded into the window opening beside him. Both Mr. Peneck and the ghost horse were forgotten.

Two of the three horses were mares which stood quietly in their stalls waiting patiently for the rain to be over. It seemed that they didn't care if they were in the meadow or in the barn.

But the third horse—the third horse—he was different. It was his impatient stamping which had startled the children. He was a sorrel with tail and mane much lighter than his hide. Although he was fully grown, their father would have called him a colt, for he was young and probably had not yet been broken.

"What a horse!" Berne exclaimed, and he didn't have to tell Amy which horse he meant.

"Berne, it's Desert!" cried Amy suddenly. "It's Desert!" Her blue eyes sparkled with excitement.

There had been many horses named Desert in the Jackson family in the last few generations, but Berne knew exactly which Desert Amy meant.

"It sure looks like him," Berne agreed, as if he had known *the* Desert well, "the way he holds his head and everything."

Amy wondered fleetingly if Mr. Peneck really did keep ghost horses in his barn.

Berne leaned out farther, and the sorrel stepped forward, lifting its head toward him. But when Berne tried to reach his nose to pat it, the sorrel snorted and stepped backward, raising and lowering his head in a rhythmic motion and restlessly pawing the barn floor with his right forefoot.

"It *is* Desert," sighed Amy. "It is, and I love him."

"I wonder how Mr. Peneck ever got a horse like Great-grandfather's?" Berne asked.

"I just can't imagine," Amy said. "Mr. Peneck certainly isn't at all like Great-grandfather. He was brave and good."

Great-grandfather Jackson's Desert had been a wonder—a beautiful, spirited sorrel with light mane and tail. Amy loved the stories about him more than any other stories that Dad told. She loved to hear her father tell how his grandfather, Arthur Adam Jackson, had bought Desert.

It happened not many years after Great-grandfather had first come into the valley. He and several other families had been the original settlers; that's why the town was named Jacksonville. He had owned a saddle horse named Tim when he arrived in the valley, but Tim had died from a fever. Great-grandfather had built a log house, cleared land, and set up a good-sized farm with the help of the team of work horses which had pulled the wagon with the family belongings across the plains. Great-grandmother had thought these work horses entirely sufficient for the work at hand. And every time Great-grandfather talked of buying another saddle horse, Great-grandmother could think of one hundred things they needed more—needles, a big cooking pot, or a new churn. Not that there was any money around to buy with in those days, but they could trade the produce from their farm for the household items they needed.

One day in late spring Great-grandfather came striding into the house shouting, "Mother, we're rich —that new gold strike in California has made us rich!"

Great-grandmother had heard rumors of California gold before, but never for one moment had she wanted to leave their valley farm to look for it.

"We're not going after gold, Arthur Adam Jackson," she said quickly.

Great-grandfather laughed. "No, but I'm going after the gold seekers."

Those who wanted gold were in an awful hurry to get it, he explained. Some had rushed off without enough provisions, and now, in the middle of their journey, were willing to pay high prices for the food they needed. Others had started with heavily laden wagons, but now that the gold fever was increasing, they wanted to get rid of their extra equipment to travel faster. They would sell for very little money things that were almost impossible to get in this sparsely settled country. So Great-grandfather planned to load his wagon with the surplus produce from the farm. One long day's drive would take him the twenty-five miles to the main trail west.

And that's just what Great-grandfather did. Great-grandmother did not expect him to return for four or perhaps five days, but after a week had passed, she was worried—what with so much work to be done on the farm, and with Indians about and neighbors so far away. Finally, on the morning of the eighth day, she saw a wagon coming slowly across the valley—very slowly, for it was afternoon before it finally crept up to the Jackson farm.

Great-grandfather, almost unrecognizable under a

heavy layer of dust, jumped from the wagon seat, gave each member of the family a big dusty kiss, then stretched up his big frame and said, "Just wait until you see what I've got."

He led them to the back of the wagon where a horse—with patches of sorrel showing through the dust—was tied.

"Here's a real horse," Great-grandfather said exuberantly.

"That?" Great-grandmother asked, terribly disappointed. "Why, he's half-starved and lame."

"I know. That's why I've been so many days coming home." Great-grandfather explained that a gold seeker had ridden the sorrel night and day with little food or water in his rush to get to California, and then he had urged the horse straight into a prairie-dog hole and lamed him. He traded him to Great-grandfather for just a little food.

Great-grandmother thought it a terrible bother that Great-grandfather had traveled so slowly to allow the lame horse to keep up. She looked in the wagon for all the riches Great-grandfather had promised he would get in exchange for their farm produce, but she could see nothing. Great-grandfather said a little sheepishly that he just couldn't see folks go hungry, even if they were so foolish about gold as to start after it unprepared. Neither had he the heart to charge them enormous prices.

So he had given most of the food away and charged so little for the rest that he had come home with only a few coins in his pocket and the lame horse. Yes, the lame horse—the sorrel with the light mane and tail—the sorrel that he named Desert after the sparkling red sands of the desert that fringed his valley home—the sorrel that did so many wondrous deeds that even Great-grandmother often remembered the day Great-grandfather had come striding into the house saying, "Mother, we're rich," with a smile on her lips and thankfulness in her heart.

The stories about Desert had been Amy's favorites all of her ten years, at least all of the ten years she could remember. To actually see a horse just like her imaginary picture of Desert excited her so that her mind ran off in wild dreams of the great deeds she and this beautiful horse could accomplish.

"Oh, Berne," she sighed, "I do love him."

"He's a beauty," Berne replied.

Although the children hadn't noticed, the sky outside had brightened and the rain had slackened to a slight drizzle. The sorrel noticed though, for he pawed more impatiently than ever in his stall and finally left it to stand in the doorway. In a matter of minutes the rain stopped. The young horse plunged into the open. He scattered the mud of the barnyard with his hoofs, trotted onto the damp meadow grass, then galloped around and around in circles with his head high and his light tail and mane streaming behind him. Much less exuberantly the two mares followed him.

Berne and Amy scrambled from the hayloft, ran through the saddle room and stalls to the big barn door from which they could view the whole meadow. They stood silently and watched the sorrel circle wildly, each with his own special dream.

"Some day I'm going to ride that horse," Berne said with determination.

"What horse?" came a gruff question from somewhere behind them.

The children spun around to see the silhouette of a big man in the door of the saddle room. Mr. Peneck, Amy thought, Mr. Peneck!

The big man walked by the stalls and came toward them. Amy held her books tightly and wondered if they ought to run for it out the barn door and through the mud. But Berne didn't move, so she stayed too.

"What horse?" he demanded.

"That sorrel," answered Berne, "the young one."

"The young sorrel?" Mr. Peneck asked gruffly.

"Yes, yes—Desert," Amy blurted out, trying to help Berne.

"Desert? Desert?" Mr. Peneck repeated, a little more gruffly.

"That's just what we call him," explained Berne. "We mean the sorrel with the light tail and mane. We've been watching him."

"Desert?" snorted Mr. Peneck. "His name is Duncan."

"Duncan!" exclaimed Amy in dismay. She forgot for a moment just how afraid of Mr. Peneck she was. "Oh, it can't be!"

"Why not?" boomed Mr. Peneck. "Why not?" He looked straight at Amy for the first time. Then Amy remembered how frightening Mr. Peneck was.

"Well, he . . . he . . . he doesn't look . . . look like a Duncan," she muttered. "He is too . . . too . . . too *wondrous*." She didn't know where the word "wondrous" came from, but she was glad it came, because it seemed to please Mr. Peneck.

"He is wondrous," said Mr. Peneck, just a trifle less gruffly. "Too bad I have to sell him."

"Sell him?" asked Berne.

"Yes, sell him," Mr. Peneck boomed. "I'm selling my horses this fall. I'll be gone this winter. There's no

use feeding horses expensive hay just to stand around in a barn. They're all fine horses. I'll need good buyers for them."

Berne shuffled his feet restlessly. His eyes shifted from Mr. Peneck to the sorrel.

"Would you sell him to us—the sorrel I mean?" Berne asked boldly.

Amy was startled by the question. She held her breath waiting for Mr. Peneck either to laugh, or to say, "To you kids?" But Mr. Peneck did neither. He stared thoughtfully out at the horse.

Finally he asked, "You're the Jackson boy, aren't you?"

"Yes, sir," Berne replied.

Amy was unable to keep still another minute. "Oh, sir, we do love him."

"Well, I will sell him to you," the man said thoughtfully. "He will cost you one hundred dollars, and he's worth twice that much. "I'll be leaving the first day of September. You can have him then."

Mr. Peneck acted as if the deal was settled and closed, but Amy wasn't so sure. Now that he said they could have the sorrel, she wondered what her mother and father would say. She knew that ten- and twelve-year-old children just didn't go around buying horses for one hundred dollars.

But Berne seemed sure of himself. "Thank you, Mr. Peneck, thank you." Then he said in a grown-up voice, "I will come over to discuss the final details in several days." He explained, too, very rapidly, how he and Amy had come to the barn to get out of the rain, but Mr. Peneck had turned to a big grain bin and was lowering a bucket into it, his mind already busy with other things.

"Well, good-bye," Berne said. "Come on, Amy."

Amy followed Berne into the saddle room. "Good-bye, Mr. Peneck," she called back toward the grain bin, but Mr. Peneck was lifting out the full bucket and didn't answer.

Chapter 2

"But what do you think Mother and Dad will say?"
Amy asked Berne as they walked rapidly toward home.
Berne was taking such big strides that Amy had to
hurry to keep up.

"They will either say yes or they will say no,"
Berne answered. "If they say no, we just won't get
Desert. And if they say yes, then we've got us a deal
made already."

This was just what Amy was aware of. They had
agreed to pay Mr. Peneck one hundred dollars by the
first of September. "But that's a lot of money to ask
Dad to give us for a horse."

"Sure," said Berne, "you can't get a good horse
for nothing."

Amy and Berne turned the corner to the road where they lived. Their house was on the west edge of Jacksonville. The houses were not close together here, and the Jackson farm extended from behind the yard all the way to Clear Creek and beyond.

Amy could see the big lilac bushes that marked the front of their yard. "Well, we'll soon find out whether they'll let us buy him or not."

Far down the road a little spot darted into view, stopped for a moment, then disappeared into the lilac bushes, Amy and Berne heard crystal-clear on the late afternoon air, "Here they come." The spot reappeared in the road, then bounced out of sight once more into the Jackson's yard. "Here they come," came ringing to their ears again.

"Jill." Amy thought it was nice to have such an energetic welcome whenever she came home, even if it was only from Jill, her younger sister. Jill was enthusiastic about most things, but especially about food and bugs.

The spot appeared on the road again and came toward them. It was Jill all right. She ran up, stopped right in front of them, planted both feet in the gravel, and said very loudly, "Hi!"

"Hi," returned both Berne and Amy.

Jill spun around and took off down the road at top speed, which was pretty tops for a five-year-old. She ran into the Jackson yard and shouted once more, "Here they come." Out of the lilac bushes she popped again, running back to Berne and Amy, who weren't nearly so far away this time. "Hi!" she repeated, then she darted back and called another "Here they come" to the house. Back and forth she ran with a shout on each end until Berne and Amy turned into the yard.

Berne and Amy walked onto the huge front porch and followed Jill through the doorway, in and out of which she had been running for the last minute, trying to decide whether to call "Here they come," or "Hi." Once inside with Amy and Berne, she announced grandly, "Here they are!"

"Where in the world have you two been?" their mother asked, coming into the front room from the kitchen. Before either of them could answer, she continued, "Now hurry and change, both of you. You've got to do the chores. Berne, you milk old Speck. Amy, you feed the pigs and calves. Dad won't be home until late. He's gone up Clear Creek Canyon after a load of rocks. Now hurry." Their mother disappeared into the kitchen.

Berne shrugged his shoulders at Amy as he hurried off to his room to change. This just wasn't the time to ask about buying Desert, Amy thought, as she climbed the stairs to her room.

Jill popped in the door after her. "I'll help you feed the pigs, Amy."

Amy hurried into her patched jeans and an outgrown shirt of Berne's and then, with her sister following, ran down the steps.

"I'll really hurry," she told her mother as she flew through the kitchen and out the back door.

Amy could see Berne already driving Old Speck into the barn. She ran into the barnyard, turned the water on for the calves and pigs, and left it running while she went into the feed shed to get the grain for the calves. She worked as fast as she could, trying to do everything just right.

Amy would have been through with her chores before Berne had finished milking if Jill hadn't dropped a bucket of feed, which she had been taking to the pigs, on the ground. Amy had to stop and pick it up. She got a little dirt mixed in when she scraped it back in the bucket, but the pigs certainly wouldn't mind that. Berne drove Old Speck out of the barn just as Amy was hanging the buckets back in the feed shed. He helped her shut the door tight and put the catch in place. They both wanted to do a good job.

Berne picked up a bucket of milk, and together he and Amy walked to the house with Jill running circles around them.

"Maybe we'd better wait until Dad comes home to ask them," Berne suggested as they stepped onto the back porch.

Berne stopped by Vacuum's dish and began pouring a little of the foamy milk from the bucket into it. Amy had named her cat Vacuum because of the way she cleaned up crumbs under the kitchen table. Vacuum dashed from around the corner of the house, leaped to the porch, and stuck her head under the last of the flow from the bucket. She crouched over her dish and lapped greedily.

In the kitchen Berne gave the milk to Mother, walked into the living room, and sat down on the couch. He picked up *Favorite Horse Stories* and began reading the story about the ghost horse, which they had started in Mr. Peneck's barn.

Amy tried to pay attention, but she just couldn't keep her mind on the story. She kept listening for the truck to pull into the barnyard. Dad certainly should be home soon now.

Their dad often went to the mountains, or all over the valley for that matter, after loads of rock. He was a rock hound, or that's what other people called him. Amy said rock man; she thought that sounded much better. He had piles of rock stacked around the barnyard, and he knew where to find anything in the whole valley—rock, plant, or animal. That's why people came to Arthur Jackson when they needed a guide. That's why Dr. Heeps came to see them almost every summer.

When Dr. Heeps came for the first time three years ago, Amy had asked him what sort of a doctor he was. He explained that he was a doctor of Zoo— something or other, which had to do with animals. Amy felt she understood, but when she called him an animal doctor, everyone laughed, especially the animal doctor himself. He said that he didn't take care of animals or make them well. When Amy asked him what he did to them then, he replied, "Well, I read about them and watch them and write about them."

Amy could see why he couldn't make animals well if that was what he did. Dr. Applegate always gave Amy a shot or thumped her chest when she was sick. Once when she fell out of the apple tree and sprained her wrist, he bandaged it for her. Dr. Applegate certainly couldn't make anyone well by writing about them, unless he wrote prescriptions. Amy asked Dr. Heeps if it were prescriptions that he wrote, but he said, "No, just books."

One day while the animal doctor was staying at the Jackson's, Hurley Thick had hit Vacuum with a rock. Vacuum was a kitten then and hadn't yet learned to stay away from Hurley and his little brother, Winston. She just lay down on the sidewalk and began to cry. Berne said that cats cried like that when they died. Amy had picked Vacuum up in her arms and cried too. Then she had remembered the animal doctor.

She thought if she told him how Dr. Applegate did things, maybe he could make Vacuum well. Amy found him behind the barn sitting on a board looking at a dead rockchuck. For a minute when Amy saw the rockchuck lying there dead, she thought she had better not ask the animal doctor to help Vacuum. But Vacuum cried again the way dead cats do, so with tears running down her face, she had asked him anyway. She couldn't even tell him how Dr. Applegate did things, she was crying so hard.

The animal doctor looked at Vacuum and said she would be all right. From his pocket he took some little straight sticks that looked like popsicle sticks and tied them around Vacuum's leg with his handkerchief. Vacuum stopped crying and so did Amy. Amy even remembered to thank the animal doctor. She told him it was lucky for Vacuum that he had those popsicle sticks in his pocket. After that everyone called him the animal doctor, even Mother and Dad.

But Dad would be home soon, for it was almost dark.

Berne finished the ghost horse story.

Jill, who had been listening intently, pleaded, "I want to hear another one. Read me another story."

"I'm not going to read any more." When Berne said he wouldn't, he wouldn't.

Jill turned to Amy. "Please, please, please, please," she coaxed, handing the book to Amy.

"Amy," her mother called from the kitchen, "Will you set the table?"

Amy was glad to escape Jill, for she was too excited about Desert to read a story now. As Amy was putting the salt and pepper on the table, she heard the pickup pull into the barnyard and then her father's heavy steps on the back porch.

"Hi, everybody," he greeted them with a big smile as he came into the kitchen. "You should see the load of geodes I brought back with me."

Amy was glad Dad was happy. It certainly would be easier to ask about Desert.

"Wash up," Mother ordered.

Dinner was ready, and as soon as everyone had washed, they sat down to a venison roast with potatoes and gravy. Amy helped herself to a small mound of potatoes, made a dip in the middle of them, then poured gravy over them. The potatoes became little brown hills with a lake in the middle, and she could almost see the beautiful sorrel running over the hills with his mane flying, and then trotting down to the lake and dropping his head to the water for a drink. Amy wished Berne would hurry and ask Dad. It would be better if Berne asked, for he knew just how to say things and didn't get mixed up like she sometimes did. But Berne was eating his dinner in silence.

"Are ghost horses like goblins?" Jill asked, with her mouth full of gravy and venison.

"But Jill," Amy explained, "that wasn't really a ghost. It turned out to be a real horse."

"I know," insisted Jill, "but if it was a ghost horse, would it be like a goblin?"

"There aren't any goblins," Amy told her, but she knew Jill would never believe that.

"There are too," declared Jill. "There are too, and are ghost horses like them?"

"They aren't a bit alike," Berne took over. "Now be quiet!" Berne was ready to ask about Desert. "Dad, Mr. Peneck has a sorrel colt he wants to sell to someone who will take good care of it." Berne's voice was as calm as any grownup's. "He said we could have it if we wanted."

"I don't need a horse around here to take care of," Dad stated. "It takes half my time to feed the animals I've got already." He went back to his plate as if that was all there was to be said.

Amy was panicky. "It's Des—" she began.

"But Dad," Berne interrupted, "not you. We—Amy and me. Mr. Peneck said we could buy him. We would take care of him ourselves."

"You and Amy?" Dad looked surprised and so did Mother.

"Good Heavens!" said Mother, "you children buy a horse?"

"It's not a ghost horse, is it?" asked Jill, but no one paid any attention to her.

"He's really a beauty, and he holds his head high and runs like the wind," Berne said convincingly.

"Well, children shouldn't have horses that run like the wind." Mother sounded determined.

"But it's Desert," Amy blurted out, as if that explained everything.

"Desert?" asked Dad.

"We just call him that," Berne explained, "because he is a sorrel with light tail and mane."

"He looks exactly like Great-grandfather's horse," Amy said.

"Hummmmm," said Dad, "is he broken yet?"

"No, he isn't," Berne was on sure ground. "Of course, we would have to ask you to help us break him. If you did, he wouldn't be a bit wild, and Mother wouldn't have anything to worry about." Berne said this rather carelessly, but both he and Amy knew their father loved to break a good horse.

"Hummmm," mused Dad. "How much does he want for this sorrel?"

This was the very point that worried Amy. "One hundred dollars," she said, her voice squeaking a little on the word "dollars."

"One hundred dollars for a horse for children—one that isn't even broken!" Mother exclaimed.

"But he's worth twice that much," said Berne. "He's really a beauty; he's terrific; he's . . ."

"Wondrous," Amy finished for him. It had seemed such a good word when they had been talking to Mr. Peneck, but now Mother looked at her in rather an odd way.

"Mr. Peneck has good horses," Dad agreed. "He's probably worth that much all right. But we can't spend one hundred dollars on a horse for you. Fifty dollars, maybe yes, but one hundred dollars, no."

Amy's heart sank.

"We could earn it ourselves," Berne stated flatly.

That hadn't occurred to Amy. Why, yes we could, thought Amy, yes we could. "Yes, we could earn it," she said out loud.

"Mr. Peneck doesn't want to sell him until September first, so we'd have all summer to save the money." Berne sounded very official.

"I'll tell you what," Dad bargained. "I'll drop over to Mr. Peneck's tomorrow and look at this Desert, and if he's as 'wondrous' as you say, you can have him. One hundred dollars is a lot of money for us to spend for a horse or for you to earn to buy one. But we could help you out. We'll put as much money toward the horse as you earn. How would that be?"

"Fine, fine," said Berne, triumph showing in his eyes. This was a better arrangement than he had expected. He dug his fork into his food and began to gobble as fast as he could, for he was very hungry now that an agreement was reached.

"Hurray," Amy cheered. "Oh, Daddy, we love him so. Just wait until you see him!"

She looked at her plate, but the mashed potatoes looked even more like hills that Desert would like to run on and the gravy even more like a lake that Desert would like to drink from. She couldn't eat a bite.

Her father smiled at her beaming face. "My, Amy," he said, "you're wondrous yourself. But if this Desert isn't a good horse, there's no deal, you know."

"Oh, he is; he is!" Amy cried. "Just wait until you see him."

"He's a good horse all right," Berne declared, still gulping his dinner.

"Is he a ghost horse?" Jill demanded again in a loud, loud voice. This time everyone laughed.

"Of course not," Mother denied. "He's real flesh and blood."

"And we'll let you ride him, after he's broken, that is." Amy promised.

"Oh boy!" cried Jill, "Oh boy!"

It didn't matter now if Desert was a ghost horse or a real one, so long as she would be able to ride him. Ghost horses weren't a bit like goblins, anyway; Berne had said so.

When everyone got up from the table, Amy

pushed her plate aside and helped her mother clear the table. After the dishes were done, Amy went into the living room and sat on the couch next to Berne.

"So the sorrel is just like Great-grandfather's Desert," asked Dad, looking at Amy's flushed face.

"Oh, yes," Amy affirmed.

"I want a story about Desert," Jill coaxed, "about Desert."

"Could your Desert walk thirty miles on a lame foot?" Dad questioned Amy.

"Oh, yes!"

"Could your Desert warn you that rattlesnakes were near?"

"Oh, yes!"

"Could your Desert swim the Yampa River?"

"Oh, yes!" Amy was sure he could do the very things her great-grandfather's Desert had done.

"I want to hear the story of Desert swimming the Yampa River," Jill coaxed. "Please, please, please, please."

"Okay, Jill, but then you'll all have to go to bed."

So their father told them the story. Berne and Amy listened just as intently as Jill, even though they had heard it many, many times before.

One spring morning, Dad began, Great-grandfather planned a trip to Cottonwood to buy nails which were needed to begin building another room on their house. Grandfather, whose name was Arthur, too, was a small boy then, about Jill's age, and oh, he wanted to go with his father. He stood around the barn while Great-grandfather saddled Desert to ride, and bridled one of the black work horses to pack the supplies home on.

"Oh, please, Papa," little Arthur begged with tears in his eyes, "let me go too."

But Great-grandfather thought it was too long a journey for such a small boy. He felt that he would get too tired and be in the way.

"No, I won't," Arthur cried. "I promise to do just what you say. I promise."

When Great-grandfather looked carefully at the serious, tear-stained face, he relented. Arthur could go.

So very early that spring morning they rode off toward town, Great-grandfather happy because he was always happy, and little Arthur happy because he was allowed to go.

But they never got to Cottonwood!

Their father paused in his narrative and stared at a place on the wall behind Amy so long that, hoping to get him started again, she asked, "Was the Yampa River as big in Great-grandfather's day as it is today?"

"How could it possibly be any smaller?" Berne scoffed at Amy's question.

"Yes, it was as big," Dad joined in. "It was wide and swift just like today."

"It must have been hard not having a bridge across it." Amy thought it was bad enough crossing the Yampa River on the bridge. It always frightened her when she looked out of the pickup window and saw so much rushing water below.

"It was," Dad agreed, "but in Great-grandfather's day there was no bridge at all—not a bridge for wagons, not a bridge for horses, not a bridge to walk on."

"I'll bet I can wade it," Jill speculated.

Father grinned but hastened to correct her. "Not the Yampa, at least not for seventy miles. It's too deep. That's why Compton had a ferry then."

"But it couldn't have been where the bridge is now," Berne reasoned. "The canyon walls are too steep."

"Correct, Berne," Dad said. "It was downriver a couple of miles at a place where the deep gorge falls off. There the country is flat and a few willow and tamarisk trees grow from the damp soil near the bank."

Great-grandfather and young Arthur, Dad began again, made good time and arrived at the ferry early. Mr. Compton was glad to have someone to take across the river and also someone to talk to.

"I hear there's Indians about," he told Great-grandfather as he helped him lead Desert onto the ferry. Although Desert didn't like the boat, he would go on it. But the black work horse couldn't be coaxed onto the ferry, so Great-grandfather tied him near the landing, planning to pick him up when they returned from Cottonwood, which was only five miles from the crossing.

"There's always Indians about," Great-grandfather replied. "But I've always treated them well, and they never give me any trouble."

"Yes," Compton continued, "but I hear these are Indians from down South."

This was an entirely different matter, Great-grandfather knew. For while the local Indians usually stuck to their own business, the Indians from the South were often raiding parties. They would steal whatever they could get—food, horses, and children—especially children, who they would take into Mexico, where the slave market assured them a good price.

Great-grandfather helped Compton start the ferry moving across the river. He was anxious to get to Cottonwood and back now that he had heard about the Southern Indians.

About halfway across the river and a little below the ferry crossing a big rock jutted above the water, even when the water was high as it was now. The ferry was even with this rock when Desert suddenly began pawing and snorting and looking toward the shore from which they had come.

"Indians, Papa, Indians," young Arthur shouted.

And Indians there were. Five or six rode out from the willows and down to the river bank.

"They aren't local Paiutes," observed Great-grandfather.

And they certainly weren't, for two of them rode to Great-grandfather's black work horse, untied it, and led it off. The rest rode to the post where the ferry rope was tied and quickly cut it. With one end loose, the boat drifted downstream and lodged against the rock.

Compton said that it was too bad about Great-grandfather's work horse, but that it didn't much matter about the rope, because they could still get to the other shore, as that end of the rope was still intact. He didn't think he would be going back across right soon, not with Indians there.

But Desert wasn't so calm about it. He pawed at the boards with his feet and tossed his head high, looking first at one shore and then the other. Great-grandfather watched the horse for a minute, then carefully surveyed the Cottonwood side of the river. He could see nothing, but Desert still snorted and looked in that direction.

"There's something wrong there," Great-grandfather decided. "Maybe we had better stay here for awhile."

So they remained in the middle of the river, making no effort to pull the ferry to the other shore. When the Indians saw that they had lodged by the rock, they shot a few arrows toward the ferry, but it was too far away to hit.

"I wonder why they want us to go to the other shore so badly?" Great-grandfather asked.

"It does seem suspicious," Compton agreed.

Suddenly another small band of Indians rode out of the willows and down to the river bank on the Cottonwood side. They must have thought that Great-grandfather and Compton knew they were there, so they came into the open and went to the tree where the other end of the ferry rope was tied.

"They're going to cut it," yelled Compton.

But Great-grandfather wasn't watching the Indians now. He was busy. He grabbed young Arthur, walked to the edge of the ferry, said, "Here you go," and lifted him onto the big rock that stood in the middle of the river.

"All right, Arthur," he ordered very firmly, "you stay there and don't move until we come after you. You must!"

"I promise, I promise, I promise," young Arthur called from the rock.

"He talked just like Jill," Amy interrupted.

"Be quiet," Berne ordered. "Let Dad finish."

By now the Indians had cut the remaining ferry rope, Dad continued, and the boat, with nothing to hold it, was jerked away from the rock into the current of the swift river and was carried rapidly downstream.

Arthur watched as the ferry with his father, Mr. Compton, and Desert was swept farther and farther away from him. Soon a turn in the river channel completely hid the boat from his view. He turned to watch the Indians to see what they would do now. The bands on both sides of the Yampa swung their horses around and rode up the banks and into the willows. For a long time young Arthur watched the trees where the Indians disappeared, but they never came back.

He crouched on the rock hugging his knees, the spray of the turbulent water making him wet and the rock slippery. He watched the water speed by the rock, and he watched the sun climb in the sky. He watched, and he waited. The only things that moved were the water and the sun. The water moved rapidly, but the sun moved slowly, ever so slowly.

But it finally touched the western hills and dropped behind them. Soon it was dark, very dark, and Arthur no longer could see the river, but, perched there on the rock so close to it, he could hear the rushing water. He was cold and he was sleepy, and sometimes he would doze a little with his head on his knees. But mostly he just waited.

Suddenly from out of the darkness he heard someone calling, "Arthur!" He sat straight up and listened, and this time the voice seemed closer, "Arthur!"

"Papa!" he shouted.

And it was Great-grandfather, for the next moment his strong arm pulled Arthur from the rock and held him on Desert. Soon they were on shore and safe.

Great-grandfather and Compton had been swept a long way downstream through the rapids before they had managed to get the boat to shore. By the time they had ridden back to the ferry crossing, it was long after dark. Since they had no boat, Compton thought they had better see if they could get one, and look for young Arthur in the morning. It was too dark to see all the way to the rock. Although they called, the rush of water drowned out their voices.

Great-grandfather knew there were no boats any-where near, and that the Indians might very well show up again in the morning. He sat on Desert at the edge of the water, wondering if young Arthur had stayed on the rock and if the family at home were safe. While he was trying to decide what to do, Desert lifted his head and neighed. He pawed the ground and shook his head back and forth looking out over the river. Soon he stepped into the calm water near shore. Then, care-fully feeling his way, he walked farther into the river.

Compton shouted, "Come back, Jackson!" for he thought Great-grandfather was urging Desert into the river.

Great-grandfather called back, "Desert knows what he's doing."

Soon they were in deep water, and Desert began swimming. Although Great-grandfather never knew how the horse did it in the dark and against the swift river current, Desert swam straight to the rock. And he made it back again, carrying both Great-grandfather and little Arthur, although they reached the shore a bit downstream from the ferry landing.

So that was how Desert became a hero to the Jackson family—and to the whole valley for that matter.

When Dad finished the story, the children went straight to bed, for when their father said bedtime, he meant it; that they all knew.

Amy didn't think that she would sleep at all because of the excitement about Desert. She did lie awake for awhile imagining what it would be like to own such a wondrous horse as Great-grandfather's Desert had been, and as their Desert was going to be. But finally she dropped off to sleep, and all night long Desert galloped through her head in water and wind and rain doing heroic deeds.

Chapter 3

"If Jeannine would only come home," Amy said in dismay as she walked along the hot sidewalk.

Jeannine Billings was Amy's best friend and had called Amy on the telephone just after lunch. She had told Amy of a family on her street who wanted to hire someone to weed their garden. After she finished the lunch dishes, Amy had rushed right over to the Jenkins' and asked Mr. Jenkins if she could weed his garden for him. Mr. Jenkins had eyed her suspiciously for a moment, then walked ceremoniously down his steps and across the lawn to the corner of the house. He pointed to the back yard where the lawn ended in a cement patio and barbecue pit. "I haven't planted a

garden for eight years." Then Amy realized that somehow she had gotten the names mixed up. When Amy
walked to Jeannine's house to ask her the correct name,
she found that Jeannine had already gone to Cottonwood with her family.

Jeannine always talked so fast that it was difficult
to understand everything she said, and then too, Amy
never could remember names. She sat down in the
shade under the box elder tree and thought about
Desert. Desert, their beautiful Desert! For he would be
theirs on September first.

About mid-morning when Dad had returned from
Mr. Peneck's, Amy was at the pickup almost as soon as
it stopped. He opened the door and smiled down at her.

"Did you like him, Daddy?" she asked.

"You certainly picked a beauty," he said, "and
Desert's a good name for him too. Mr. Peneck will
bring him over the first day of September."

Amy hadn't waited to hear more, but gave a
squeal of delight, and ran off to tell Berne. She found
her brother sitting on his bed thumbing through a
sports magazine.

"Dad liked him, Berne," Amy had squealed, and
she jumped up and down a couple of times because she
couldn't help it.

"Sure he liked him," said Berne, shutting the
magazine and looking closely at the cover. "I knew he
would. All we've got to do now is to earn fifty dollars."

But Berne's calmness didn't rub off on Amy. She
danced through the house all morning until Jeannine

had called. Amy thought that weeding was a wonderful way to begin earning money for Desert. But now she had forgotten the name and would have to wait for Jeannine to come home to find out.

Soon Amy heard the sound of whistling from up the street. Sweet and clear came the tones of "The Old Chisholm Trail."

Berne had gone over to the east side of town this afternoon to mow lawns. He had been mowing two lawns there every Saturday, but today he had hoped to find others that he would also be able to take care of all summer. It would be a beginning of the money which they needed to buy Desert.

Amy noticed that he was whistling "The Old Chisholm Trail," not "I'm an Old Cowhand." Even though he usually came home from the east side with two or three shiny quarters, he was not quite·happy enough to whistle "I'm an Old Cowhand," because he had to mow two or three lawns to get that much money. It wasn't that Berne didn't like to work. He could work harder and faster than any other twelve-year-old boy in all Jacksonville. It was just that the lawns he mowed belonged to the new folks on the east side. Since the dam had been started at Cottonwood, lots of new folks had moved into Jacksonville and had built a new section of homes on the foothills and into the canyon mouth. They were nice folks, but their lawns were different—not at all like the Jacksons' lawn which was broken by clumps of lilac and iris, with sweet peas and morning glory growing near the fence.

The east lawns had all those prickly shrubs and flowers with fancy names that Amy couldn't even pronounce. They sounded like combines to her.

But worst of all the east lawns were either uphill or downhill, so they were very difficult for Berne to mow. He sometimes started at the top, hung on tight to the mower, and leaned as far back as he possibly could. Then he zoomed down the lawn. Usually he could stop before he got to the middle of the street. Of course, he had to make sure no cars were coming before he started down. He could mow a lawn very quickly this way. Except once he zoomed down so fast that he mowed a clump of those fancy combine flowers. The lady didn't like that at all, but she gave him a quarter anyway. So Berne usually mowed up the lawn instead. This was much slower, but at least he could stop when he came to the combine flowers. Sometimes, too, the ladies would give him an extra dime because he worked so hard.

Berne stopped whistling when he saw Amy under the box elder tree. He walked across the street into the shade by her.

"Berne," Amy burst out, "I can't find the right place."

"What right place?" Berne asked tolerantly.

"That Jeannine said needed weeding—a garden, I mean," Amy explained.

"Oh, Jeannine, huh?" Berne mumbled, as though that explained any confusion that ever happened. "Do you want to see what I've got?" he asked, suddenly changing the subject. He thrust his hand into his pocket, pulled it out, and opened it slowly.

"For Desert," he announced.

"Oh, Berne!" Amy exclaimed, "you earned six quarters!"

"That's a dollar-fifty," he said, "and every one of the people that I mowed for wants me to work every Saturday, so that's a dollar-fifty I'll make each week."

Oh, that'll be enough to buy Desert!" Amy said enthusiastically.

"Not nearly enough," corrected Berne, "but it'll be a good start. Counting this Saturday, there are just twelve before September first, so that makes eighteen dollars from mowing lawns. We'll have to think of some other way to earn the rest of the fifty dollars."

"I'll earn some too," said Amy, and she really meant it, for surely when Jeannine came home, Amy would be able to find whose garden needed weeding.

"Good." Berne walked from the shade to the hot sidewalk. When Amy didn't follow, he turned back expectantly.

"I'm watching for Jeannine to come home," Amy explained.

"Jeannine," Berne slurred. "You can call her from home. Mother said she wanted us home early this afternoon to get ready for the Pioneer Day Program."

Amy reluctantly left the shade and joined Berne as he walked down the sidewalk. "I guess it will be too late to weed a garden this afternoon anyway."

When they arrived home, Mother had a whole list

of jobs for Amy to do. In the midst of her duties, however, Amy managed time for several telephone calls, but no one answered at Jeannine's house.

"I guess I can ask Jeannine at the Program," Amy told Jill as she buttoned the back of her dress. Jeannine was to square dance with Amy and the rest of her class.

After Mother straightened Amy's hair and retied her sash, they joined the rest of the family in front of the house. She and Berne walked side by side down the street toward the school auditorium. Mother and Dad were just behind them. Jill was in front of them— sometimes *just* in front of them and sometimes a *long way* in front of them, depending at which end of running back and forth she happened to be. When Jill was a long way down the road, Mother called, "Jill, please wait a minute." Jill turned around and ran back to them, only to start running in the other direction again.

When they reached the school grounds, Berne went to the music building to get his trumpet. The rest of the family went into the auditorium. Jill ran to the very middle seat of the first row. Her mother and dad sat down next to Dr. Applegate in the row behind her.

Amy looked around for Jeannine. Almost everyone Amy knew was there except Jeannine. Suddenly a push from behind sent her into a row of folding chairs, which tumbled together with a terrible racket. Amy landed on the floor. Hurley Thick bent over her laughing.

"Have you seen Jeannine?" asked Amy, as she got

up from the floor and started putting the chairs back in a row.

"Naw." Hurley got all set to push her again.

Just then Miss Applegate, Amy's teacher, took Hurley by the shoulder and made him sit down; then she helped Amy put the folding chairs back.

"All the square dancers will have to sit on this side by the stage door," said Miss Applegate, looking down her long nose at Amy. "I think everyone is here except Jeannine." Miss Applegate looked down her nose just the way Dr. Applegate did when he thumped Amy's chest. Miss Applegate was Dr. Applegate's daughter. She wasn't very old really; she just looked that way. That was probably why she wasn't married.

"Hi," Amy greeted Michael Carbunkle as she sat down on an empty chair next to him.

"Good evening," Michael replied. Michael had lived in Jacksonville only a year. His father was an engineer for the Cottonwood Dam. He always wore a bow tie, a jacket, and shiny shoes. Even though he was a head shorter than Amy, he was her square-dancing partner, for Amy was one of the shortest girls in her class.

"Amy Pamy is a damy," chanted Hurley as he sat down on a chair on the other side of Michael.

Hurley had nicknames for almost everyone. Amy Pamy wasn't as bad as his nickname for Jill. He called her Jilly-jelly. But Hurley didn't have a nickname for Berne. No one ever called Berne anything but Berne. Berne's full name was Berne Arthur Jackson, and from the sound of it, he could be a President of the United States or an animal doctor or anything. Amy wished she had an important sounding name like that. Her name was just plain Amy—Amy Jackson. She had always wished it were Elizabeth Margaret Ann Jackson. That would sound more important. Besides Berne was named after things. Father had been a soldier in Berne, Switzerland when he had written to Mother asking her to marry him. So Berne was named after a city in Europe, and of course Arthur was Dad's name and Grandfather's name and Great-grandfather's name too.

"Amy Pamy is a damy." Hurley reached behind Michael and pulled a strand of Amy's blonde hair.

"Quiet," said Miss Applegate. "Quiet!"

The program was beginning.

"My dear ladies and gentlemen," began Mayor Todd. He always called everyone "dear." "Tonight we are here to honor the settlers of this fine town." Then he began talking about Arthur Adam Jackson and his little log cabin by Clear Creek. Amy covered her ears as the Mayor spoke, for he made her Great-grandfather sound very dull—almost silly. Amy knew her Great-grandfather wasn't at all like that. He was good and brave—especially brave.

After Mayor Todd spoke, Berne played his trumpet, because he was a descendant of the first settler. Berne played his trumpet at almost every program in Jacksonville, even when it wasn't Pioneer Day. Playing the trumpet was easy for him, like whistling.

Jill from her seat on the front row said in a loud

voice, "Hi, Berne," twice before Mother could quiet her.

Throughout the long program Amy watched in vain for Jeannine to arrive. When Miss Applegate whispered, "It's time to line up now for the square dance—quietly," Amy decided her friend was not coming and gave a hopeless sigh as she thought of the weeding job.

The group of square dancers didn't line up very quietly, however, for Hurley pushed everyone on the way, but they reached the stage door just as Sarah

Todd, the Mayor's teen-age daughter, said the last verse of the Little Orphan Annie poem about the goblins.

Sarah singsonged, "You'd better mind your parents and your teachers fond and dear, And cherish them that loves ya and dry the orphans' tears, And help the poor and needy that clusters round about, Or the goblins will git ya, if ya don't watch out."

"They won't get me," Jill boomed in her cat-calling voice to Winston Thick, who was sitting by her. "They won't get me," she said loudly to Dr. Applegate behind her. This time she shook her head slowly, so there would be no mistake. "They won't get me," she told her mother, who was leaning forward trying to quiet her.

Miss Applegate put the square dance record on the phonograph. "Without Jeannine here the boys will just have to dance with the air," Amy said to herself as the children walked backstage, "unless they dance with Miss Applegate." She hoped not. Miss Applegate would look awfully funny swinging with Michael Carbunkle.

Amy felt someone pushing behind her. She grabbed the curtains that covered the back of the stage and held tight, afraid that Hurley would push her out on the stage all by herself. But the pushing stopped. She looked around and found that it hadn't been Hurley at all, but Jeannine trying to get to her place in line.

"Oh, Amy." Jeannine was all out of breath, "I was almost late."

"Jeannine, Jeannine," began Amy, "who was it that . . . ?" But Amy didn't have time to finish, for the square-dance music started. They all ran onto the stage as the caller on the record said, "And they cut down the old pine tree."

The dance started. "Bow to your partner," chanted the caller. This was the part Amy liked best. She curtsied daintily. Michael hinged up and down like Jill's windup toy, a mechanical man. "Swing your partner, swing your corner." Hurley was Amy's corner and when he swung her she held tight to his sleeve so she wouldn't sail across the stage when he let her go.

When Amy passed Jeannine as she circled the square, she whispered, "Whose garden was it?"

Jeannine looked back at Amy. "What?"

"Whose garden was it?" Amy mouthed.

Jeannine made a face to show that she couldn't hear.

There were lots of bows and swings before Jeannine passed Amy when she circled the square.

"Whose garden needed weeding?" Amy tried again as they came close together, but she could see that Jeannine still didn't understand.

As they passed each other, Amy asked once more in a quiet shout, "Whose garden is weedy?"

This time Jeannine heard. She pointed into the audience and said loudly, "Sheriff Jensen's."

Sheriff Jensen! Why, of course!

Amy looked across the square at Jeannine to let her know that she understood. She was startled to see her friend hurry off into the other square of dancers and try to swing a boy who already had a partner. Amy was so surprised she forgot to hold tight to Hurley's sleeve when he swung her, and when he let go, she went sailing across to the front of the stage. She stopped with both feet dangling over the edge looking straight into Jill's eyes.

Without Jeannine and Amy their square became a mass of confusion. Hurley almost swung Michael, but the caller on the record saved him with the last, "And they cut down the old pine tree." The music stopped.

The applause was tremendous. Amy sat on the edge of the stage watching everyone clap. They all looked so funny, Amy thought, laughing so hard. Amy scrambled to her feet and joined the other square dancers as they left the stage. The clapping grew louder as they walked into the auditorium.

But Jeannine wasn't thrilled with their success.

"You didn't need to ask me right in the middle of the square dance and get me all mixed up," she stormed.

"But I've been looking for the garden ever since you called," Amy explained. However, she had to admit to herself that after waiting all day to talk to Jeannine, a few minutes more wouldn't have made any difference.

"Well, it was dumb anyway," Jeannine insisted.

"I guess it was," said Amy. "I'm sorry, but, oh, Jeannine, Desert will be ours on the first of September, and you can have a ride on him as soon as he is broken."

Jeannine, somewhat pacified, went off to find her parents.

Amy pushed through the crowd to the row where Sheriff Jensen had been sitting, but he was nowhere in sight. She looked wildly about, hoping to see his light brown cowboy shirt. After a moment, at the other side of the auditorium near the piano, she caught a glimpse of a light brown shirt. She hurriedly wound her way among the chairs and groups of chattering people. She excused herself for stepping on one lady's toes and said, "I'm sorry," for bumping into Mrs. Jenkins. As she moved on toward the piano, she heard Mrs. Jenkins complain about the children nowadays, and she was glad the Jenkins didn't have a garden.

Finally she reached the piano and looked around hopefully for the brown shirt. There it was—the back of it—just at the other end of the piano. She slid along the wall and tapped Sheriff Jensen on the elbow.

"May I weed your garden?" Amy asked.

Sheriff Jensen turned around. Only it wasn't Sheriff Jensen. It was Mr. Jenkins. He stared at Amy very hard for a long moment, then said very loudly, "Listen, kid, I don't have a garden."

Amy stepped back very quickly. She bumped into two men behind her, then fell between them to the floor. She peered between one man's legs at Mr. Jenkins. "I'm sorry," she explained. "I guess I made a mistake." But Mr. Jenkins was busy talking to several adults again.

"Are you all right?" she heard a voice and looked up to see Sheriff Jensen bending down to help her.

"Oh, yes." She scrambled to her feet. "May I weed your garden?"

"So you want to go to work?" Sheriff Jensen questioned, smiling at her.

Amy nodded. "To earn money to buy a horse."

Sheriff Jensen still smiled. "My garden is weedy enough, that's for sure. But I got word today that my brother, Jimmy, is coming in on the bus in the morning. He'll be here four or five days. He's an expert gardener. I'll tell you what. You come around a few weeks after he has left and we'll probably have more weeds by then. Okay?" Sheriff Jensen patted her shoulder.

"Okay," Amy replied. She tried not to look disappointed, for she wanted to start earning money for Desert now, not in a few weeks. She had counted on weeding that garden. She hurried away through the crowd, avoiding the piano and Mr. Jenkins.

Amy found Mother, Dad, and Jill waiting for her by the door.

"You looked very comfortable sitting on the edge of the stage," Dad teased.

"They won't get me!" Jill said emphatically.

"They won't get me!" Jill repeated to Berne as he joined the rest of the family.

"Who?" asked Berne.

"The goblins won't!"

It was a beautiful moonlit night as the Jacksons walked down the road toward home. Berne and Amy were together in front. Just behind them was Jill between their mother and dad. Everyone was thinking about the summer ahead, and each was busy with his own plans for it—all but Jill, that is. She had other things to think about.

"They won't get me," she said. "They won't get me." And she said it all the way home.

Chapter 4

"After she wears her stockings once, she just throws them away and buys new ones," Jeannine told Amy. "That's how rich she is."

"Just throws them away?" Amy asked. She couldn't imagine anyone that rich.

"Yup, just throws them away," Jeannine stated. "She doesn't wash them or anything. Just takes them off and throws them away." Jeannine was telling Amy about a wealthy girl she had heard of in Cottonwood.

"Well, if I were that rich, I wouldn't just throw good stockings away," said Amy. "I'd spend my money on something else."

"Like what?" asked Jeannine. "She has everything."

"She doesn't have Desert," replied Amy. "If I were that rich, I would spend my money on Desert."

Amy and Jeannine were sitting in Jeannine's coal shed, each holding a small kitten on her lap. School

had been out for the summer for a week now, and this morning Amy had walked over to Jeannine's house, hoping Jeannine could think of some way to earn money.

"Don't you know anybody who wants a girl to do house work or anything?" asked Amy.

Jeannine thought for a moment. "No, but why don't you go up Foothill Road and knock on each door and ask the ladies there if they need anyone to baby-sit?"

"I did," said Amy. "I went all the way up to Carbunkle's house yesterday. Some of the ladies said they would call me if they needed help, but not one of them wanted help now. And I went down First Street where there are lots of gardens and asked if I could weed, but no one wanted his garden weeded. Everyone thinks I'm too little. I'm sure they don't believe that I'm ten. It's terrible to be so short."

"There are plenty of other ways to earn money," Jeannine said.

"But how?" Amy asked. When Jeannine didn't answer, Amy continued, "I promised Berne I would earn some. He's made lots of money mowing lawns already, and Mr. Orson told him that he can unpack boxes at the store on busy days. Berne thinks he can get Billy Jensen's paper route too when Billy quits. But Desert will be part mine, so I'll just have to help pay for him!"

"If I needed money, I would make something and sell it," announced Jeannine positively. "I'd sell it up-town where there are lots of people."

"What could I make?"

"Lemonade!" Jeannine said without doubt. "It's hot now; if I needed money, I'd sell lemonade."

Amy thought about it for a moment. "But where would I get the lemons?"

"Buy them." Jeannine figured anyone would know that.

"But I don't have any money."

"Lemonade would be just the thing to sell," Jeannine was determined.

"Maybe I could make some bead jewelry." Amy suggested an alternative idea. "I have billions of glass beads." Amy had received three bead hobby kits for Christmas last year; one from Berne, one from Jeannine, and one at the school Christmas party. Then her grandmother had sent her another one for her birthday in February. Amy had threaded glass beads on several wires that were included in the kits to make necklaces, but they stood out stiff and looked funny, so Amy had put the beads in bottles and wound the wire around some empty thread spools, then put them all away in her closet.

"Yes," Amy decided, "I'll make bead jewelry."

"Well, *I'd* sell lemonade," Jeannine stated, a little annoyed that Amy hadn't adopted her idea.

"Come over to my house and help me make the bead jewelry," Amy pleaded.

"All right," Jeannine finally consented.

The girls put the kittens back in the box and hurried the five blocks to Amy's house. When they went upstairs to Amy's room, she brought out her bottles of glass beads and spools of thin wire. She really did have a lot. Jeannine and Amy sat on the bed and poured the beads in a little dent they made in the bedspread, then sorted out the various colors.

First they made rings—blue, red, yellow, orange, white, and green rings. Then they made blue and yellow rings, red and white rings, green and orange rings, and multi-colored rings. Some were single, made from one circle of wire, and some were double, made from two circles of wire. For the single rings they decided they would charge three cents and for the double rings five cents.

"Why don't we make flowers now?" asked Amy after she counted seventeen single rings and twenty-one double rings. "That's probably all the rings we can sell today anyway."

"It would be easier to make lemonade." Jeannine was tired of threading the small beads onto the wire, but when Amy showed her how to make flowers, she decided to help.

They made flowers by covering a long wire with beads and fastening the ends together to form a circle. Then they bent the wire toward the center in five places and fastened the middle with a small piece of wire. They worked until they had eighteen flowers. For the small flowers they would charge five cents; for the middle-sized flowers they would charge seven cents; and for the large ones they would charge ten cents.

Still more beads were left.

So they made necklaces—necklaces of many colors —just four of them, for they had finally used all of the beads. For the necklaces they decided to charge fifteen cents.

It took them quite awhile longer to make the

price tags. Amy tore sheets of her notebook paper into small squares, while Jeannine wrote the prices on them. Amy gathered the jewelry and tags together in a box, and the girls went downstairs.

"Mother," Amy called toward the kitchen door, "may I go uptown with Jeannine for awhile?"

Her mother gave her permission, but told the girls to have some lunch first, for it was nearly one o'clock. Amy and Jeannine each made a cheese sandwich. Just as Amy took a bite of hers, Jill popped in the door.

"What are you eating?" she wanted to know, looking longingly at Amy's sandwich.

"A cheese sandwich." Amy showed Jill.

"Can I have one?" Jill asked.

"Okay." Amy made a cheese sandwich for Jill—a big one, for she knew how hungry Jill always was.

When she saw Amy start for the door with the box of bead jewelry, Jill asked with her mouth full, "Where are you going?"

"Just uptown," said Amy nonchalantly. She and Jeannine tried to hurry off before Jill could ask the next question, but they weren't fast enough.

"Can I go too? Can I go with Amy, Mother?"

"I think it would be all right," Mother consented.

"But Jill!" Amy gave Jeannine a helpless look, "We'll be busy, awfully busy!"

"I'll help," said Jill. She followed them out the door and through the yard.

"You'll have to do just what we say," Amy ordered sternly.

Jeannine had an idea. "We can use her for a display. We'll need to show off the jewelry."

Jill didn't know what display meant, but it sounded exciting to her. The girls walked quickly to town with Jill running along beside them.

"Where would be a good place to sell the jewelry?" Amy asked. "How about in front of Orson's Store? Lots of people go there."

"In front of the post office would be a better place. Everybody comes to the post office to pick up mail," Jeannine argued.

Amy saw at once that the post office would be the best place, for Mr. Orson sold jewelry in his store and might not like it if Amy put up a stand by his door.

First, however, they stopped at Orson's, and the clerk was glad to give them some cardboard packing boxes—two very large ones and three smaller ones. These they hauled across the street and dumped on the sidewalk in front of the post office. They stacked the two large boxes together and arranged their wares on top.

While Jeannine put the price tags in the appropriate places, Amy crossed out the words CRACKERS on the front of the boxes with a black crayon. With a red crayon she spelled out in big letters BEAD JEWELRY. The girls put the three small boxes behind the big ones to sit on if they got tired.

Their counter complete, they stood behind the boxes and looked up and down the street. No one was coming.

"I want to be a display," said Jill, hoping that it was something fun to be.

"Okay," said Jeannine. She put a small box in front of the counter. "Sit here."

"Do displays have to sit down?" asked Jill.

"Yes," said Amy, "and they have to sit still."

Jill was beginning to suspect that being a display might not be so exciting after all, but she obeyed. Jeannine put five rings on Jill's fingers, and pinned two flowers to her blouse and two in her hair. For a finishing touch, she fastened a necklace around her neck. Jill was quite excited to find herself decorated with so many colored beads, but she sat as still as she could anyway.

Amy and Jeannine returned behind the boxes to wait for their first customer. They looked up and down the street for quite awhile, but still no one was coming.

Jill began to wiggle. First, she wiggled only her fingers to watch the sun sparkle on the rings. Since no one was coming to see the display, she thought it wouldn't matter if she bent over to look for ants in the cracks of the sidewalk. But she didn't see any, so she leaned back and stuck both feet up in the air. She held her arms straight out too, trying to balance on her little box without holding on.

She balanced very well for awhile, but a car went by in which there was a dog that barked out the window at her. Jill got so excited she forgot she was a display and put her feet higher in the air. Suddenly she tipped backwards, falling hard against the counter.

The boxes tipped over, scattering the jewelry and the price tags all over the sidewalk.

"Oh, Jill!" Amy scolded, "just see what you've done."

Jill was very sorry, for she knew that good displays should never spill the merchandise. She worked very hard to help Amy and Jeannine pick up everything and put it into place again. Amy moved the display box away from the counter, so that if the display tipped over again, it wouldn't upset the jewelry.

Again they waited a long time before Jeannine pointed up Foothill Road and said, "Well finally, here comes someone!"

Sure enough, up Foothill Road was a dot, and it was coming down the hill toward Main Street. The dot grew slowly until it was the shape of a small boy, and the shape of a small boy grew slowly until it was Michael Carbunkle. Michael turned into Main Street and walked toward them. The three girls watched his every step as he came near. Even the display sat very still.

"How do you do," he said stiffly when he came near them. That was the way Michael talked.

"Fine," replied Amy. She never knew whether to say, "Fine," when Michael said, "How do you do," or just to pretend he had said, "Hi."

Michael didn't look at their jewelry. He walked by the cardboard counters without slowing down and turned into the post office. Amy looked at Jeannine with surprise. "He didn't even notice our jewelry!"

"I'll bet he'd rather buy lemonade," Jeannine reasoned.

Soon Michael emerged from the post office with a couple of letters in his hand and started past the girls on his way home.

"Michael," Amy was desperate, "did you see our pretty jewelry?"

Michael stopped and looked at the rings, flowers, and necklaces.

"We made it ourselves," said Amy.

"It is very nice," Michael spoke stiffly, smoothing out his pants, even though they weren't wrinkled.

"I'm the display," announced Jill, twisting sideways so she could look up into Michael's face.

"I'll bet your mother would like a flower," Amy encouraged. "We have all colors."

"Yes," said Michael, "perhaps she would." But he didn't offer to buy one.

"Would you like to buy one for her?" Amy asked hopefully.

"Yes." Michael spent a long time deciding which one he wanted. Finally he picked out a big red and white one and gave Amy a dime. Without another word he turned away and started up the street.

"Come again," Amy called after him.

That's what the clerks at Orson's Store always said when she left. Amy kissed the dime, then held it up for Jeannine to see.

But now they had to wait again, this time even longer than before. Several grownups came by, but they didn't stop to look at the jewelry. Mayor Todd said, "Hello, girls," and Miss Applegate nodded at them. There were a few people whom Amy didn't know very well, and there was one stranger—a dark man who shuffled by and looked at them out of the corner of one eye. Amy and Jeannine were tired of waiting.

"Everyone would buy lemonade on such a hot day," Jeannine said.

Amy stared forlornly at her jewelry.

The display was very tired. She would stand up and sit down and lie over the box on her stomach. But when she went crawling off down the sidewalk following a stinkbug, it was too much for Amy. She took all the jewelry off Jill. They would have to do without a display.

It was hot—terribly hot. Amy and Jeannine took turns going into the post office to get cool.

Finally they had their second customer. It was Sarah Todd, who came up to the boxes asking, "What are you two doing here?"

"Selling jewelry," Amy answered.

"Hey, it's clever," admired Sarah, picking up a middle-sized flower.

Jill ran back up the sidewalk when she saw they had a customer. "I'm the display," she said, forgetting she no longer was wearing the jewelry.

"I'll buy this flower," Sarah told Amy as she handed her seven cents.

That was all the customers the girls had all afternoon. Hurley and Winston Thick came by in their patched jeans, but they certainly weren't customers.

Hurley said, "What ya doin' here, Amy Pamy?" When Amy told him she was selling jewelry, he said, "That stuff's jewelry?"

He grabbed three bead flowers, then ran off down the street, hoping Amy would chase him.

"You bring those back, Hurley," Jeannine shouted angrily with her hands on her hips.

She would have run after him, but Amy told her that Hurley would bring the flowers back if they just ignored him. Sure enough, after awhile he returned and threw the jewelry over the counter at the girls saying, "Here's your pretty peonies." Then he went into the post office.

Winston sat down on the curb by Jill, who was

watching a potato beetle crawl along the gutter. After a moment he reached down, caught it, and held it close to Jill.

"Now this bug will get you," he told her.

"Bugs can't hurt you," Jill said unafraid.

"Yes, they can," argued Winston. "They climb and climb and climb on you; then they eat you up."

"Bugs can't eat you up," said Jill. "They don't have big enough stomachs."

Just then Hurley came back out of the post office. Winston jumped up and, still holding the beetle, joined his brother as he strolled up the street.

Jill shouted after him in her loud, loud voice, "You give me back my bug."

"It's not yours; it's mine."

"I was watching it first."

But Winston didn't bring it back. Jill spent the rest of the afternoon looking for another one. Although she found a daddy-long-legs, some ants, and one more stinkbug, she never did find another potato beetle.

"We've only made seventeen cents all afternoon," said Amy to Jeannine as they watched the Thicks walk up the street.

"Jewelry just doesn't sell," Jeannine remarked. She had known it wouldn't.

"Remember when Hurley made five dollars once in just a minute," Amy sighed.

Jeannine remembered, and so did every other kid in town. It was probably the only time in his life that Hurley had ever had more than a nickel at once. One of the big high school boys had told Hurley he would give him five dollars if he would eat a worm. So Hurley did—ate it right down without blinking. But Amy didn't think she could eat a worm, even for Desert.

They had no more customers that afternoon and just as they were gathering up the jewelry to go home, Berne came along. He surveyed their set-up for a few moments, and then said, "If you think you're going to make any money that way, you'd better think again."

"Lemonade would be better," Jeannine mentioned hopefully.

"Ha!" Berne snorted, "you have to sell something people want to buy."

Amy was very discouraged by the next afternoon when Michael came by again on his way to the post office. This time he bought a seven-cent flower. However, Amy knew Michael couldn't buy all the jewelry, and he was their only regular customer. Several grown-ups had been by again, but they hadn't even glanced at the stand or the girls, except for the strange dark man who looked at them out of the corner of his eye.

"Oh, Jeannine," sighed Amy, "we'll never earn enough money this way."

Jeannine agreed, for she still thought lemonade would sell better. "If no one would buy lemonade, at least we could drink it ourselves. It is so hot!" Jeannine mopped the perspiration from her neck.

It was Jeannine's turn to go into the post office to get cool. She was there a long time, and Amy was hoping she wouldn't be much longer, when suddenly

Jeannine came leaping down the steps looking excited.

"Amy," she cried, "we've got five hundred dollars. Come and see quick!"

She dashed back up the steps to the post office and inside before Amy could ask her what she meant. Amy decided it would be all right to leave the jewelry stand for a minute since there was no one on the street except herself, so she walked into the post office. There was Jeannine bustling back and forth in front of the bulletin board where a lot of pictures were tacked. When Amy came up to her, Jeannine pointed excitedly to a poster that had **$500 REWARD** printed on it in big letters. The poster contained two pictures, one of the front of a man's face and one of the side. Underneath in big letters was the name, Michlo Tippiana. Amy carefully read all the printing on the poster, but she still couldn't understand why Jeannine was pointing excitedly at it.

"We'll share the reward," planned Jeannine. "Now all we've got to do is to tell Sheriff Jensen." She hurried to the door of the post office.

Amy still didn't understand. "Tell him what?" she asked Jeannine as she caught up with her in the doorway.

Jeannine didn't answer. She stood frozen in her tracks staring out at a man who was coming down the street toward them. It was the strange dark man they had seen pass their jewelry stand several times.

"That's him," Jeannine whispered breathlessly. "That's Michlo Tippiana."

He did look a little like the picture, Amy thought. He had dark hair, bushy eyebrows, and a big nose. Then too, the way he shuffled down the street, looking at everything sideways, was suspicious. As Amy watched him, he stopped at their jewelry stand, then instead of giving it a look out of the corner of his eye, he turned his head and stared directly at it. Amy remembered that the poster had said Michlo Tippiana was a thief— a jewel thief. She wondered if he were going to steal their bead jewelry. But he must have decided not to right then, for soon he continued on by. He shot them a sidelong glance as he passed the post office door. Jeannine trembled, and Amy had an uneasy feeling that perhaps he knew that they knew.

"Come on," said Jeannine nervously after the man had disappeared from view, "let's find Sheriff Jensen, quick!"

She rushed up the street toward the court house. As Amy followed her, she wished that they had brought Jill with them today so she could watch the jewelry stand while they were gone.

As they walked quickly, they looked carefully in the windows of each store and around the corners of each building, half expecting to see the strange dark man jump out at them.

Finally they reached the court house, went through the big doors and down the hall, carefully reading the name by each office. In the middle of the hall on the second floor they found a door marked SHERIFF. It was open, so they peeked in. No one was there.

"Let's wait for him," Jeannine decided.

Amy readily agreed for she didn't want to walk back up the street where the jewel thief could jump out at them from behind the buildings. They stood in the doorway and waited for ten minutes, which seemed like ten hours, before they heard footsteps on the stairs.

"This must be Sheriff Jensen now," Amy whispered.

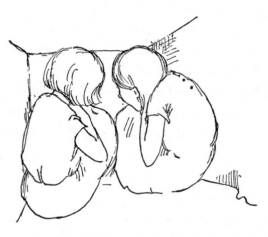

They both looked toward the stairs. The person coming toward them wasn't Sheriff Jensen at all, but the strange dark man.

He must have followed us here, Amy thought in panic. Without a word the girls quickly tiptoed into the office and crowded under Sheriff Jensen's desk. It was terribly close with both of them there, but they managed to peek out the crack under the desk, through which they could see the floor of the hall.

A pair of black shoes came into view and stopped right in front of the sheriff's door. Amy could almost feel eyes looking through the wood of the desk. Her spine felt prickly. The black shoes came into the room and up to the desk. Then they turned and one swung up out of view. It bumped the desk making such a sudden bang that both Jeannine and Amy jumped, although there really wasn't much room for jumping where they were. The strange man sat down on the desk.

Amy hoped that he didn't know they were there, that he was just waiting for them to come. He seemed to be very patient, for he sat there fifteen minutes, whistling quietly to himself. That was the longest fifteen minutes Amy had ever spent. Their hiding place seemed to grow smaller and smaller. Amy began to itch, first here and then there, and then everywhere, but she didn't dare move to scratch.

Finally both black shoes appeared on the floor again and walked out of the room.

"Maybe we'd better wait here a minute to make sure it isn't a trick," Jeannine whispered.

Immediately they were glad they did, for they heard footsteps in the hall. The footsteps came in the sheriff's door, up to the desk and right around behind it before Amy and Jeannine could move. This time the footsteps weren't made by black shoes, but by high brown-and-white cowboy boots.

"Well," exclaimed Sheriff Jensen in astonishment as he peered down at the girls crouched under his desk. "Well."

The girls scrambled out from under the desk as

rapidly as they could. Amy bumped her head twice in the hurry.

"We found him," Jeannine announced.

"Under my desk?" asked the sheriff, looking in each of the girls' hands to see if they were holding a dog or a cat or something that could be called a him.

"Oh, no, he's out there." Amy nodded toward the hall. She wondered fleetingly how the strange man could possibly have been under the desk with them. There just wasn't room.

The sheriff stared at them. When Amy and Jeannine merely looked back at him, he finally asked, "Who?"

"Michlo Tippiana," Amy said, surprised that the sheriff didn't know who they had found. The poster had said that all the police were looking for him.

"Michlo Tippiana?" repeated Sheriff Jensen.

"Yes, on the poster!" Jeannine explained desperately. She was afraid the strange man would come back before the sheriff knew what they were talking about.

"Poster?" echoed the sheriff.

He pulled open a drawer and took out a stack of posters like the ones the girls had seen in the post office —each one with a picture of a different person on it. He held them up one at a time. Somehow all the faces on the posters looked just the same to Amy now, so she carefully read the names under the pictures until they came to the one marked Michlo Tippiana.

"That's him," whispered Jeannine, glancing cautiously out in the hall.

"You saw this man?" asked the sheriff.

Jeannine nodded emphatically, so Amy did too.

"Where?" questioned Sheriff Jensen.

"On Main Street," replied Jeannine, "but he followed us here."

"We saw his shoes last in the hall," Amy added.

The sheriff walked into the hall. "Hey, Jimmy,"

he called in a loud voice, "come here a minute. Did you see a man like this in the hall?"

"Nope," said the man who followed the sheriff back into the office.

Amy and Jeannine gasped with terror. It was the strange man with the dark hair, the bushy eyebrows and the big nose—the man with the black shoes—the strange man they had seen on Main Street.

Jeannine just pointed at him speechlessly, but Amy managed a whisper, "That's him."

"Him?" asked the sheriff.

"Me?" asked the dark man.

The sheriff and the strange man looked at each other. First they smiled, then they merrily slapped each other on the back.

Amy was puzzled, "Why are you laughing?"

Sheriff Jensen only laughed harder, but finally he sobered enough to tell them that this man wasn't Michlo Tippiana at all, but Jimmy Jensen, his very own brother, from up north who was visiting for a couple of weeks. Both Sheriff Jensen and his brother began to laugh again.

Although Amy didn't think the whole affair was quite as funny as the men did, she did think it was funny, so she laughed with them. Jeannine didn't think it was funny at all. She grabbed Amy's hand and tried to hurry out of the room.

"Good-bye, Sheriff Jensen and Mr. Jensen," Amy called over her shoulder as Jeannine pulled her out the door.

"I'm going back downtown," Mr. Jensen said. "I'll walk with you." And he did.

He was very nice and told them about the time he had mistaken a stranger for a friend. When they got back to the jewelry stand, he bought three double rings and three big flowers to give to his cousins and gave Amy forty-five cents for them.

That forty-five cents was the beginning of a good

afternoon for Amy, for soon Jake Wilkins, one of Berne's adult friends, came along, stopped and bought thirty-five cents worth of bead jewelry, although he didn't have little children to buy it for because he wasn't married. He told Amy, winking his eye, that it was for his girl friend.

But the biggest sale of all came when a tourist lady stopped at the post office to mail some cards.

"Oh, how cute," she said when she saw the bead jewelry sign.

"We made it ourselves," Amy explained.

"Oh, how cute. What are you going to buy with all the money you make?" The lady giggled to herself.

"Desert," Amy answered.

"The desert!" exclaimed the lady. "Oh, how cute."

"No, Desert. He's a horse."

"Oh, how cute," said the lady again. She bought two necklaces, two big flowers, two small flowers, two double rings, and two single rings. She gave Amy seventy-six cents.

That was the last day Amy sold bead jewelry on Main Street. Although she still had some left, she gave most of it to Jeannine for helping her, and she gave some of it to Jill too for being the display. She kept two flowers and a double ring for herself.

Since Berne thought Amy wouldn't be able to make any money selling bead jewelry, he was very sur- prised when she gave him a dollar eighty-four to put in the box where they kept their money for Desert.

Chapter 5

Ring went the Jacksons' telephone. *Ring, ring, ring.*

The telephone hadn't been working for a few days, so a repairman had come to fix it. First, he would come in the house with his screwdriver and take the plate off the telephone box, then he would go outside and climb the telephone pole. That is when the ringing would start. Soon he would climb down from the pole and return to the house with his screwdriver, then out he would tromp and up the pole he would go again.

Jill, Amy, and Berne watched him climb the pole until he frowned at them every time he passed them on his way between the telephone and the pole. So Amy decided she would go in the house and forget about the repairman.

But this was hard to do with the telephone ringing constantly. Finally she decided that he wanted someone to answer to see if the phone worked. So she picked up the receiver and said, "Hello."

The man said, "Little girl, please hang up the phone."

Amy hung up. After that she pretended she couldn't hear it. But it was very hard for her to ignore the noise. After the phone rang for what seemed to Amy to be hours and hours, she began to wonder if the repairman had finally finished and if Jeannine were calling about weeding the gardens in her neighborhood. Jeannine had promised Amy that she would ask all the people on her street if they wanted two girls to weed their gardens for them. She said she would call Amy if they did. Amy wondered too if one of the ladies up on Foothill Road might be calling her, for some of them had said they would if they needed a baby-sitter.

The telephone sounded again. Amy ran to answer, "Hello."

"Now listen, little girl . . . " said the repairman.

Amy hung up as fast as she could and ran into the kitchen to get a carrot to chew on. Maybe she wouldn't be able to hear the telephone ringing when she chewed on a carrot. When she found she could, she went out on the back porch to sit with Berne.

Berne was whistling "The Old Chisholm Trail" and looking at the cover of a hunting magazine with a picture of a gun, a hunting cap, and a stuffed bird stacked together on a table.

"That's a nice picture, don't you think?" Berne asked Amy.

"Ummm," mumbled Amy, chewing harder on the carrot.

"That bird is the sort of thing that tourists would want to buy."

"Well, I don't know," said Amy. Bead jewelry seemed to Amy to be just the thing for tourists to buy, yet even that had been very difficult to sell.

"Of course they would want to buy stuffed birds. They come to this part of the country to see the mountains and the rocks and sand and birds. So sure they would want to buy stuffed birds," Berne argued.

"Maybe," Amy conceded.

"Of course they would like to buy stuffed birds, because they look so alive, but sit so still. And they are no trouble at all. You don't even have to feed them." Berne thought how pleased he would be when a tourist said, "Oh, isn't it really alive?" and he would say, "No, I stuffed it myself."

Just then Jill came around the corner of the house singing. "Hum de dum, hum de dum. I'm singing a pretty cowboy song," she said to Berne and Amy. "Hum de dum, hum de dum."

"Do you want to come with me to get a bird?" Berne asked.

"Yes, yes," Jill answered. Berne had really asked Amy, but he didn't mind Jill coming along too.

"Are you going to Jake's?" asked Amy, not quite sure she wanted to go.

Jake Wilkins had a hobby of taxidermy. His place was full of stuffed birds. Amy sometimes went there with Berne, but she didn't like to. Birds looked down at her from shelves and dressers and cupboards. Amy wondered if Jake had offered Berne his extra birds to sell. He certainly had plenty of them.

"Only for a minute," Berne replied. "Jake said he would give me some thread, wire and stuffing when I got ready to stuff a bird myself."

"*You're* going to stuff a bird?" Amy was a little startled. "You—yourself?"

"Sure," Berne replied nonchalantly. "You and Jill pack us a lunch while I ask Mother if we can go up to the foothills into the oaks. I'll get our bikes and my pump gun too." He disappeared around the corner before Amy could answer.

"Oh well," she said to Jill, "if we're only at Jake's for a minute." She liked going to the oaks, where there were squirrels and lizards and all kinds of birds.

The telephone rang all the while she and Jill fixed the lunch and it was still ringing when they rode off down the road on their bicycles. As they pedaled along, Berne explained that Mr. Porter had said he could sell stuffed birds at his gas station if he wanted. Mr. Porter's station was just north of town on the main highway. Lots of tourists stopped there to buy not only gas but also cards, film, Indian jewelry, and other souvenirs. They also stopped to see the mountain lion which Mr. Porter had in a cage. Mr. Porter had named it Thunder because that was how it roared. Yes, Mr.

Porter's gas station would be a good place to sell stuffed birds.

Jill took turns riding on the handlebars of Berne's and Amy's bikes. She only knew how to ride a tricycle, and that would be too slow to go all the way to the oaks.

Amy had the lunch in the basket on the back fender of her bicycle. Berne had his pump gun tied behind him. Berne could shoot his gun very well. Jeannine had scoffed when Amy told her Berne was the fastest gun in Jacksonville. But it was true. He could pick it up, pump it, and bang—hit anything he wanted before you knew what he was doing. Amy knew because she had been rabbit hunting with him. Since rabbits ate the farmers' crops, everyone liked Berne to hunt rabbits. Mr. Porter would give Berne five cents apiece for them; he needed them to feed Thunder.

But Berne didn't go around shooting birds—not usually. In fact, Amy had never seen Berne shoot one. Hurley Thick did though. He would sneak around with his gun and bang up into the trees. Mostly he would miss because he couldn't afford a pump gun and only had a broken down B.B. gun. But once in awhile he would hit one. Then he would stick it in his pocket, so that he would have a dead bird on hand with which to chase Amy if he happened to see her.

When the three children reached Jake Wilkins' place, they saw Dr. Applegate's car in front of the house.

"I hope Jake isn't sick," said Berne.

He wasn't. When Berne knocked on the door, Jake answered it, wearing about the biggest smile Amy had ever seen.

And Dr. Applegate wasn't there at all. Miss Applegate was. She had just made an apple pie, she said, and happened to think how well Jake liked apples, so she had brought it over to him. No wonder Jake was smiling, thought Amy, as she looked at the apple pie. It would have made her smile too if it hadn't been for the huge stuffed hawk which was looking at the pie from its perch on the refrigerator.

Of all Jake's stuffed birds, the hawk filled Amy most with wonder. Its eyes stared right at you; its wings were spread out; its left claw was raised, and its beak was wide open. The first time Amy saw it a squeal came out of her mouth without her even knowing it was coming. But Jake thought she had squealed because she liked it. "Nice, huh!" he said. After that Amy always tried not to look at the hawk. Berne and Jake often ate apples in front of the bird, but not Amy. She just wasn't hungry when she was at Jake's house, and she didn't wonder that Jake was so skinny with that hawk staring at him every time he went to the refrigerator.

"It's a mighty good-smelling pie," said Jake, still admiring his gift.

"It smells like birds in here," observed Jill, sniffing around.

That brought Berne back to his reason for coming. "I'm going to stuff a bird tonight."

"Good, good." Jake was pleased that Berne was ready to try his first bird. He gathered together some sawdust, wire, sticks, and things, and put them in a paper bag for Berne.

"It's pretty hard at first," Jake reminded Berne as they were leaving. "Just come over if you need any help."

Berne thanked Jake, and the children got on their bicycles and rode east toward the foothills. They took a lane that went through the farms on the south side of town. Both sides of the lane were lined with tall poplar trees, and irrigation water ran in ditches in the fields where the alfalfa was already a foot and a half tall. Often when they passed farm houses, two or three dogs would run out to the road and bark at them, but they always ran back to the yards when Berne called to them.

Soon the children left the farms behind and started the climb through the sagebrush and junipers into the canyon mouth. Here Clear Creek emerged from the mountains, bringing water of melting snow from the highest peaks into the dry valley below. It was too steep to ride the bicycles here, so they got off and pushed them.

"I wish we had Desert now," Amy shouted to Berne who was far in front of her and Jill. "We wouldn't have to get off and push him."

Berne stopped to wait for them. "Of course we wouldn't have to push him. It's silly to even think of such a thing. Desert can walk right up these steep hills without even becoming winded, just like Great-grand-father's horse could do."

"I know we wouldn't have to push him," puffed Amy. "That's what I said."

But Berne was thinking of his Great-grandfather. "Like the time they came up here looking for the cows that wandered off."

"And the snake bit Great-grandfather," Jill added as she ran along holding onto the back fender of Amy's bike.

It was true, Amy thought; Great-grandfather had been up in these very foothills hunting for missing cattle. Near dark on his way home with the strays, he shot a couple of sage hens. He swung off Desert to pick them up, intending to leave the horse standing with the reins hanging, as he usually did. But Desert wouldn't stand. He snorted impatiently and pawed the earth; he swung his head in the direction where the sage hens lay, and tried to walk the other way after the cows. Desert had never done this before, but Great-grandfather reasoned that the horse was anxious to get home because it was dusk. So he tied the reins with a good knot to a branch of a small oak with Desert pull-ing at the reins the whole time.

Great-grandfather climbed through a steep gully and was about to the place where the sage hens lay when almost under him he heard a rattling noise which could only mean one thing—a rattlesnake. He jumped for a large rock, but wasn't fast enough, for the rattler struck, sending its deadly poison into Great-grandfather's leg just above his big boots. The rattler quickly slipped off into the sagebrush and rocks.

Great-grandfather pulled his pantsleg up and tied his hankerchief around his leg above the bite. He cut into his flesh with his knife and sucked out as much of the poison as possible. Then he lay as still as he could, for he decided with rattlesnake poison in him it would be very unwise to over-exert himself by climbing through the gully to reach Desert.

Jill had been tossing attractive rocks from the road into the basket on the back of Amy's bike, and now the collection was so heavy that Amy stopped to empty them out while her sister protested loudly. Berne stopped too, rolling a juniper frond between his hands as he waited.

"It was sure lucky for Great-grandfather that he was riding Desert that day," Amy commented.

"That's for certain," Berne reflected. "If any other horse had broken the bridle reins, it would have taken off toward home like a streak of lightning. But not Desert!"

But not Desert! Suddenly Great-grandfather realized that Desert was near him in the darkness. Although dizzy and weak he pulled himself onto Desert's back and lay there while Desert carried him home. Great-grandfather was very ill when they reached the ranch, and as Great-grandmother and the boys lifted him from Desert's back, it began to sprinkle a little. A few minutes later the rain poured down in a storm the like of which this country seldom saw. The next day

the mud was so deep that some of the animals were
bogged down, and later several adobe sheds on the
farm began to melt away.

"Great-grandfather would have died from expo-
sure if Desert hadn't brought him home," Berne said.
They had left most of the juniper trees below them and
now the scrub forest consisted mostly of oaks.

"It was Desert who saved his life," Amy gasped for
breath, for the climb had been steep.

"Desert, Desert," Jill chanted with several puffs
between each "Desert."

Amy wanted to call "Desert, Desert" along with
Jill, but she didn't because she was much too old for
such five-year-old nonsense, so she let her heart sing it
silently.

Desert, a horse just like Great-grandfather's,
would soon be theirs.

Here the road was narrow and bumpy, and they
could hear the chatter of squirrels back in the timber.

"This will be a good place," Berne decided. They
left the bikes by the side of the road and cut off
through the bushes. Amy carried the lunch while
Berne carried his gun.

"All right, now, be quiet," ordered Berne.

"I'm hungry," Jill complained.

"We might as well have our lunch now," said
Berne. They sat down on the green bank of Clear
Creek to eat. The air was wonderfully cool. Across the
stream some squirrels scampered up a tree.

A blue dragonfly settled on a damp rock for a

moment and then flew away. Amy remembered that she had been afraid of dragonflies when she was Jill's age. Hurley Thick had told her that dragonflies were just like needles and they would sew up her mouth if they caught her. So Amy had always run away from them. Now Amy knew that Hurley had just been teasing her. Winston had told Jill the same thing about dragonflies, but Jill wasn't afraid. She had caught too many to believe a story like that. Besides the only things she was really afraid of were goblins.

Jill and Berne finished eating their sandwiches, but Amy could only eat half of hers, so she wrapped up the other half and put it in her pocket.

As Berne picked up his pump gun, ready to move on, from a tree across the stream came a clear, beautiful call, "cleee—ip." All three children paused and listened. "Cleee—ip," came an answer from a tree over their heads. Berne peered through the branches of the tree.

"Maybe we had better not . . . " began Amy.

"Quiet," whispered Berne.

"Cleee—ip," came the call over their heads again.

Berne raised his gun.

Bang! Berne stood with his gun still raised as the bird crashed through the branches of the tree, landing in front of him on the ground. It was a beautiful yellow and black grosbeak. For a moment there was silence.

"Oh," said Jill, "Oh!" Then she opened her mouth terribly wide and out came the loudest noise in all the oak country. That was the way Jill cried.

From the tree across the stream they heard the call again, "Cleee—ip." It was the mate calling, but this time there was no answer. Amy tried hard not to let the tears spill down her cheeks.

Berne picked up the bird at his feet. "Well, I got my bird," he said, but he didn't sound very happy.

"Cleee—ip," came the mate's call again. A squirrel hidden in the branches of a tree began to scold. Crows below them in the junipers began to caw. "Cleee—ip," came the mate's call again.

Amy just couldn't keep back the tears.

"Girls!" said Berne in disgust.

He started toward the bicycles. Jill and Amy got up to follow him. Both were crying, although Jill had quieted some. Amy remembered the sandwich in her pocket. She took it out, unwrapped it, and set it at the foot of the tree for the grosbeak's mate. She hoped the bird would get it instead of the squirrels who were scolding from the tall oak.

As they walked back to their bikes, all the creatures of the oak country seemed to scream after them. The squirrels kept up their noisy scolding, and the crows flew up from the junipers cawing hoarsely. A roadrunner fled from the path awkwardly twisting its neck and angrily clicking its bill at them. But the worst sound to Amy was the "Cleee—ip, cleee—ip," of the grosbeak, calling for its dead mate. The tears blurred her eyes, and she could hardly see where she was going.

Jill stopped for a moment to look at a lizard that was sitting on a rock. It stretched its head up toward her, opened its mouth wide, and hissed. Jill began to howl afresh.

When they reached the bicycles, Berne was already tying the bird and his gun on the back of his bike. "You ride with Amy," he ordered Jill. "You're too noisy for me."

As they started down the mountain, Berne rode off in front of them. He said he didn't want to be drowned by all those sissy tears. But Amy noticed that he didn't whistle at all on the way home, not either one of his favorite tunes.

No one mentioned the bird again. And at supper when Mother asked them how everything was in the oaks, Berne mumbled, "Oh, about the same."

Berne spent that evening and the next day out by the barn working on the bird, trying to make it look alive again. He used all the thread and sawdust that Jake Wilkins had given him. When it was finished, he brought it in the house and set it on the dresser in his room. Both his mother and dad said it was a pretty good job for the first time.

Berne was sitting on his bed with his head to one side looking at his bird when Amy came into his room and saw it. She couldn't imagine anyone wanting to buy it, for it looked ragged and droopy. She pretended she hadn't seen it, borrowed the colored pencils she had come after, then left.

"At least it isn't on the refrigerator," she said to herself.

A little later Jill walked into Berne's room looking

for Vacuum. When she saw the bird sitting on the dresser, she opened her mouth wide, took a deep breath, and let out a howl that seemed to shake the whole house. Everyone in the family came running to see if she had fallen out of a window or stuck her finger in a light socket.

"Goodness, Jill," her mother exclaimed, "what's the matter?"

"What's that dead bird doing on Berne's dresser?" Jill asked between howls.

"Just sitting there," said her dad.

"It won't hurt you," Mother explained. "It's dead."

"I know it's dead," howled Jill. "Dead things shouldn't be sitting on Berne's dresser."

"But Berne stuffed it, just like Jake Wilkins does." Mother glanced at Berne anxiously.

"It's not like Jake Wilkins' birds," Jill insisted, and it really wasn't. "It's all floppy and dead looking . . . like . . . like . . . like a goblin."

"Berne did pretty well for his first bird," said Mother. She led Jill, who was still howling, to the kitchen. Everyone left Berne's room and Berne shut the door. Amy thought he probably didn't want to look at the bird either.

Soon Jill stopped crying and went out to play. When Mother called her for supper, she came in covered with dirt and smiling from ear to ear. Dirt and smiles usually went together for Jill. Mother sent her to the bathroom to wash, but when she returned to the kitchen, her mother took one look at her, said, "Good heavens," and marched her right back to the bathroom.

Berne was the last one to come to the table. He sat down and asked quietly, "Where's my bird?"

Everyone stared at Berne in surprise, everyone, that is, except Jill, who was looking very hard at the fried potatoes.

"Is it gone?" asked Dad.

"Yes, it's not on my dresser."

"Maybe Vacuum . . . " began Amy.

"Jill!" Mother looked straight into Jill's eyes the way she sometimes did when she knew something you didn't want her to know.

"I'd like some fried potatoes," said Jill.

"Jill Jackson!" her mother spoke very firmly.

"Dead things shouldn't be sitting on Berne's dresser," Jill insisted.

"Jill, you must never take things that aren't yours. You get Berne's bird and put it back on his dresser," Mother ordered.

"I can't."

"You can't?"

"At least, I can't very easy."

"Why?" asked her mother. "What did you do with it?"

"I buried it!" Jill looked at Berne to see how angry he was, but he didn't look cross at all. "Dead things should be buried."

"After supper you go out and dig it up," commanded Mother, "and put it back where you got it."

"Well," Berne said slowly, "that's all right. It doesn't matter. Anyway I wouldn't want Jake to see it. I mean, after it has been buried, it might not look so good. Well, that's all right, Jill." Berne reached for the fried potatoes.

Amy was quite relieved that it had turned out this way.

As they ate supper, Mother talked to Jill about things that were hers and things that didn't belong to her, and how she must never take things that weren't hers without asking permission from the person who owned them. "Do you understand?" Mother asked when she had finished explaining.

"Uh-huh," said Jill. "I'd like some more fried potatoes."

Berne handed her the fried potatoes. Jill smiled at him, and he smiled back at her.

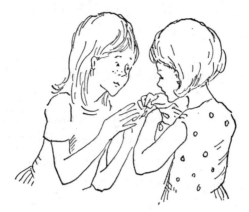

Chapter 6

"I'll read you a book, but not that one," said Amy, "not *Amelia Anne Stiggins*."

"Oh, please," coaxed Jill, "please, please, please, please, please."

Amelia Anne Stiggins, which had been a Christmas present from Mother, was Jill's favorite book. Jill would listen to it as often as she could get anyone to read it. She liked it because in the end Amelia got to eat so many cakes and cookies and other goodies. Jill wondered what it would be like to eat so many goodies all at one time.

"Please, please, please, please," Jill continued.

"Okay," Amy gave in, "but I'm only going to read it once."

"Oh boy!" Jill sat down as Amy began to read. The story was about a little girl, Amelia Anne Stiggins, who was invited to a party given by the rich man of the town for all the poor children. Amelia's brothers and sisters were invited too, but they couldn't go because they had colds. So when Amelia Anne got to the party, she put all her goodies in her umbrella instead of eating them so she could take them home to share with her brothers and sisters. The rich man had a sister who didn't like children, and she discovered the goodies in Amelia's umbrella. She was very angry. But the rich

man discovered what had happened and gave Amelia Anne a huge basket full of goodies to take home for herself and her family. They ate them at the end of the book. That was the part Jill liked.

"I sure wish you would read it again," Jill pleaded, "but I guess you won't."

"No, I won't, because I just don't want to."

"Why?" asked Jill. She couldn't understand anyone not wanting to read *Amelia Anne Stiggins.*

"Because it has that nervous old woman like Mrs. Jenkins," Amy answered, "and because I have to think of a way to earn some money."

Amy wished that she was rich like the man in *Amelia Anne Stiggins* or the girl in Cottonwood who threw away her stockings after wearing them just once. This morning Amy was especially worried about the money they needed to buy Desert. She hadn't earned any all week, and Berne had made only a little hunting rabbits for Mr. Porter and unpacking boxes for Mr. Orson.

Berne and Amy had taken out their box this morning to see exactly how much money they had. Berne counted it while Amy sorted out the little slips of paper on which they had written how the money was earned.

"Twenty dollars and fifty-two cents," Berne had announced soberly after he finished counting.

"That's not half enough," Amy had said.

"If I were only thirteen, I could have Billy Jensen's paper route soon," Berne lamented.

There were so many slips of paper that Berne helped Amy add the numbers on them. Berne had earned nine dollars mowing lawns, two dollars and ninety cents hunting rabbits for Thunder, and two seventy-five helping at Orson's Store. Amy hadn't earned nearly as much as Berne, only one dollar eighty-four selling jewelry, three dollars and a quarter weeding gardens for Sheriff Jensen and several others, and seventy-eight cents collecting deposits on pop bottles with Jill.

But now the summer was half over, with only six weeks until September first. By that time they would have to have fifty dollars. Amy just couldn't think of another way to earn money. She planned to go up and down the roads on each side of town looking for pop bottles. But as for selling jewelry again, she didn't think there was much use, and the gardens she had worked in were now weedless.

Amy walked in the kitchen to ask her mother if she could go to the other side of town to look for pop bottles. When the telephone rang, she dashed back to the living room, but Jill was nearer the phone and got there first.

"Hello." Jill listened for a minute and then said, "Amy, it's for you. It's a lady."

"Hello," said Amy into the telephone receiver.

"Is this Amy Jackson?" asked a lady's voice.

"Yes," Amy replied.

"This is Mrs. Anchor. I live up on the east side of town. I need some help with the children today. I have so much cleaning to do. Mrs. Carbunkle gave me your name and said you would be a lot of help. Do you think you could come for a couple of hours?"

"I think so," said Amy. Mrs. Carbunkle was Amy's Bluebird leader, and Amy had always stayed to help her clean up when they had parties.

"My house is on Foothill Road, two blocks east of Main Street. It's a gray cinder-block house."

"I'll find it." Amy was imagining the money she would be able to earn for Desert. She was just going to say she would ask Mother if it would be all right, but Mrs. Anchor hung up.

Amy found Mother mixing bread in the kitchen. When Amy told her about Mrs. Anchor's call, her mother said she could go, but to be sure to be back by three o'clock to stay with Jill while she went to Relief Society.

"Good-bye, Jill," said Amy as she left the house.

"Mrs. Anchor didn't say Amy *and* Jill, did she?" Jill called with her nose pressed against the screen door.

"No," Amy answered as she rounded the lilac bush. "Just Amy."

"Well, good-bye then," she heard Jill say from inside the screen door.

The animal doctor, who had arrived at the Jacksons' the previous evening, was changing a tire on his pickup in the shade of some big poplar trees by the apple orchard that separated the Jackson's and the Thick's yard.

"I'll give you a ride uptown as soon as I get this tire changed," he told Amy when she stepped into the street.

"It's not very far, thank you," Amy said. She didn't want to wait for the animal doctor because if someone came along, Amy might be hours getting to Mrs. Anchor's, for the animal doctor loved to talk.

The animal doctor planned to be with the Jacksons for the rest of the summer. He was finishing a study of prairie dog diseases. Then he planned to study spotted skunks. Amy couldn't imagine why he wanted to study spotted skunks. No one ever brought skunks to a doctor or prairie dogs either for that matter.

Amy was wondering so hard about prairie dogs and skunks that she forgot to walk to the other side of the street before she came to the Thick's yard.

"Yoodle-dee doodle-dee dooooooo—," sang out Winston, who saw her first.

"Well, if it ain't Amy Pamy," said Hurley.

He and Winston were sitting on their unpainted front porch, eating watermelon. They would take a bite, seeds and all, chew for a minute, then spit the seeds into a grassless spot near the steps.

"Hello." Amy walked faster.

"Here, have some watermelon," Hurley snickered as he threw what was left of the rind at Amy.

It went sailing by her and landed in the middle of the road. Winston, trying to finish his watermelon so he could throw his rind too, gobbled so fast that he swallowed a whole mouthful of seeds.

"I swallowed some seeds!" he exclaimed.

"Ha ha ha!" laughed Hurley. "We can have watermelon every day when vines grow out of your ears."

He thought this was so funny that he lay down on the lawn and rolled over with laughter. While Winston sat on the porch worrying about watermelon vines growing out of his ears, Amy hurried on before he could finish eating his piece of watermelon.

Soon she came to the streets closer to town where there were sidewalks. When she passed Dr. Applegate's house, she thought she smelled apple pie, and she wondered if Miss Applegate was making another apple pie for Jake Wilkins.

Since it wasn't out of her way to go by Jeannine's house, Amy turned the corner onto her street. She saw the Billings' old blue car pull up and stop at the far end of the block. Jeannine and her parents stepped out and walked to their gate.

"Jeannine!" Amy ran as she shouted. "Jeannine Billings!"

Jeannine waved her arm vigorously and then dashed up the sidewalk toward Amy.

"Look," Jeannine called as they drew near each other. She held up her arm and pointed to her wrist.

"You've got a new bracelet." Amy said when they met.

"It's a *charm* bracelet!" Jeannine exploded. "I just bought it this morning in Cottonwood."

One at a time she held up the charms—books, pencils, bottles of ink, and slates—for Amy to see.

"It's nice," Amy complimented.

"*Charm* bracelets are all the rage," Jeannine enlightened Amy as the girls walked toward Jeannine's yard. "Everybody has one, even the junior high girls. Sarah Todd's charm bracelet has hearts and arrows on it."

Amy was impressed. "I wish I could get one."

"Sarah told me there was just one left at Orson's after she bought hers last night." Jeannine was glad to have convinced Amy so quickly. "I'll bet if you hurry you can get it."

"Oh, Jeannine," Amy moaned, "I can't. We're saving for Desert."

"One bracelet wouldn't matter much." Jeannine turned in her gate. "Come in," she invited Amy.

"I can't now. I'm going to help Mrs. Anchor this morning. Maybe I can stop on the way home."

As Amy crossed the street, Jeannine waved to her, looking, however, at the bracelet bobbing on her own arm instead of at Amy.

Suddenly Jeannine remembered something, ran onto the roadside and shouted, "Amy, guess what Miss Applegate is going to do."

Amy liked guessing what. She thought very hard before she called back across the street, "Make an apple pie?"

Jeannine shook her head with impatience.

"She's going to get married—to Jake Wilkins."

"Well, good," commented Amy. "I'll bet she bakes Jake a lot of apple pies when they're married."

Jeannine returned to her yard impatiently.

As Amy walked by Orson's Store on Main Street, she decided to go in and look at the bracelet just to see what it was like. She pushed open the door and walked to the back of the store between the envelopes and straw hats where the jewelry counter was. A fat lady who was looking at earrings was standing exactly in front of the counter. Amy could see the charm bracelet, lying in a small section at the back. She tried to reach it from one side of the lady to examine the charms, but it was too far to reach, so she went around to the other side of the lady. But even when she stood on tiptoe, she still couldn't reach it.

"Well——!" said the fat lady, "*ex-cuse* me, little girl!" But she sounded like she didn't mean to be polite. She moved over a little, at the same time setting her large handbag exactly over the bracelet section. Amy tried to peek under the bag, but the charms were hidden completely. Well, it doesn't matter, Amy thought, I can't buy it anyway. But she wished she could.

Amy left the store and walked up Foothill Road. It was steep here where Berne mowed lawns, and Amy could see combine flowers growing in the yards. She saw Michael Carbunkle come out of his house and walk down the street toward her. Michael had a dog on a leash, a dog that was as small and as neat for a dog as Michael was for a ten-year-old boy.

"Hi," Amy said to Michael when she came near him.

"How do you do," Michael replied. Amy decided to pretend he had said hello.

"Hi," she said again. "I like your dog." She stopped to look at it, but it frowned at her, so she didn't try to pet it.

"Thank you."

There was silence for a moment while Amy studied Michael's dog. With the dog frowning and Michael standing so quiet, Amy decided she should say something.

"Miss Applegate is going to get married."

Michael made no reply.

"To Jake Wilkins," Amy added. She waited, expecting Michael to say, "How nice," or "It's about time," or something.

Michael could see a reply was necessary, but he could think of nothing to say for a moment. Finally he spoke. "I hope they will be happy." He pulled on the dog's leash and off they went down the sidewalk.

Amy continued up Foothill Road until she was nearly two blocks from Main Street. The house just in front of her was gray cinder block. As she walked up the steep concrete steps and rang the doorbell, she heard children crying inside the house.

The lady that answered the door said, "Oh, you must be Amy. Come in. The children are driving me crazy. Take them out in the back yard and watch them while I clean up this messy house. I'm having club tonight."

It took Mrs. Anchor several minutes to gather the

children from off a cupboard, under a bed, and out of a toy box. When she had them assembled in the kitchen, they numbered four, the oldest about the size of Jill. Mrs. Anchor held the back door open while Amy herded them outside.

"Keep them in the back yard so that John and Robbie won't run out in the street." With this parting instruction, Mrs. Anchor closed the door.

"Hi," Amy said to the children, who stared at her from various places on the steps. Even though there was nothing in their appearance to give her a hint that they were boys, Amy supposed the two youngest were John and Robbie, for the two oldest children had long brown hair.

"What's your name?" Amy directed the question to the smallest long-haired child.

The girl slid off the second step and crawled behind some boxes. She peeked silently at Amy.

"Her name is Maxine," the other girl answered for her. "She's only three. I'm almost five, and my name is Kay."

"What shall we play, Kay?" Amy asked.

"Let's play pretty!" Kay decided promptly.

Now Amy had expected London Bridge, Ring Around the Rosie, or even Run Sheepy Run, but she was game anyway. "All right, Kay, you be pretty first and dance for us."

Kay put both hands on her hips and informed Amy in no uncertain terms, "That isn't how you play pretty."

"How do you play pretty then?" Amy felt a little annoyed at Kay's attitude.

At that moment the smallest Anchor, who had been slithering down the steps behind Amy blabbered, "Ah gooa mum bab," entwined both hands in her hair, and jerked rhythmically.

"Ouch!" Amy tried to pry his hands loose, but his little fists tightened and pulled harder. "Let go, Robbie! John!" Amy used both names, not knowing which one fit.

The baby let go of her hair, but at the same moment the two-year-old boy, hearing himself scolded, began to cry. Amy tried to comfort him, but he only tilted his face to the sky and sobbed to the clouds. Somehow in the confusion Amy discovered that his name was John, the baby's was Robbie, and that you played pretty with Mother's high heels, dresses, and lipstick.

Amy finally quieted John by carrying him to a patch of loose dirt and putting a toy dump truck in his hand.

She returned to the other children on the steps. Robbie was putting a rock on his head and letting it fall to the ground. Kay was swinging her arms, clapping her hands in front and then behind her back. Maxine was still behind the boxes.

"I want to play pretty!" Kay yelled.

"I'll tell you a story," Amy tried to divert her.

"I don't want a story. I want to play pretty. You promised I could. You promised."

"I certainly did not," Amy contradicted, greatly
annoyed.

"You did; you promised," Kay howled. "Mama!
Mama!"

"All right, we'll play pretty," Amy consented
crossly.

Kay stopped howling immediately. "I'll get Mama's high heels."

Amy thought fast. "You won't have to. I know a
way to make high heels that are much better."

She went to the corner of the house and began rummaging through the garbage can. Kay was curious enough to follow. Maxine's interest lead her from the shelter of her boxes. When John and Robbie joined the crowd, Amy gave them each an empty milk carton to fill with dirt.

"Here's just what we need," Amy held up two empty evaporated milk cans.

"They aren't high heels," Kay cried, obviously disappointed.

"They will be. You just watch." Amy managed to sound very enthusiastic. Laying the cans on their sides on the ground, she jumped on the centers of each.

"Hold out your foot," she ordered Kay. Amy held the can under Kay's foot and bent the sides up until they gripped her shoe.

"There!" sang Amy when she had both tin cans attached. "How pretty!"

This wasn't exactly true, for the cans didn't become Kay's feet at all, but she didn't seem to notice. She clomped off across the yard as though she were Miss America.

Amy was glad to have Kay satisfied, for at that moment John began pouring dirt over Robbie's head. Robbie stuck out his tongue and enjoyed the downpour until some got in his eyes.

"John, don't do that!" Amy grabbed the carton from his hands.

So John, who was a very sensitive boy, joined Robbie's crying.

By the time Amy wiped the dirt out of Robbie's eyes with the corner of her shirttail and kissed John five times, Kay and Maxine were fighting over the high heel cans.

"You can't have them," Kay shouted. As she pulled away from Maxine, she stepped on her finger.

Maxine sobbed, "Santa Claus will bring me some high heels, but he won't bring you any. He will bring me lots and lots of high heels because I will walk to the North Pole and tell him, because I can walk thirty miles."

"The North Pole is farther than that. It's two hundred miles or forty thousand miles and its too far to walk," Kay scoffed.

"Then I could drive a car or a tractor or something," Maxine argued.

"No, you couldn't. You would have to have flying monkeys or eskimo birds."

"I'll buy me an eskimo bird then," Maxine whined, rubbing the tears from her cheek with her fist.

At this point they had come so far from high heels that Maxine was a little puzzled when Amy took her to the garbage can and made her an identical pair of mashed evaporated milk cans.

The rest of the baby sitting time went rather well. Maxine stayed out from behind the boxes. Robbie didn't pull Amy's hair. John didn't cry when Amy called his name, and Kay became Amy's ardent admirer.

Kay was explaining to Amy that everybody has

eyebrows, even daddies, when Mrs. Anchor opened the door and asked Amy to bring the children in and bathe them. The baths turned out to be quite an ordeal, but not much worse than bathing Jill.

By two o'clock Mrs. Anchor felt she had everything under control.

"Thank you, Amy," she said as Amy was leaving. She handed her a half dollar and a quarter. "I'll call you again when I need help."

"Thank you," Amy replied politely. "Good-bye."

As she walked down Foothill Road, she thought about bracelets and wondered what charms were on the bracelet at Orson's. They might have been apples or bananas, or they might have been eggs. By the time she was in front of Orson's Store on Main Street, she was so curious about the charm bracelet that she walked into the store and back to the jewelry counter. The lady with the large handbag was gone, and Amy reached the bracelet easily.

She looked at it closely. The charms were not apples or bananas, and were far from eggs. They were footballs. Six of them were fastened to the chain and each had a word written on it. Amy read the words carefully, "Kick . . . that . . . ball . . . kick . . . that . . . ball." Amy was a little disappointed that the charms weren't apples, bananas, or eggs, but she thought the bracelet was very pretty anyway. As she was about to put the bracelet back on the counter, a clerk came up to her.

"Would you like that bracelet?" she asked Amy.

"Yes," sighed Amy, thinking how much she really wanted it even though she wouldn't be able to buy it. She laid the bracelet down and was turning to go when the clerk picked it up, put it in a paper bag, and rang fifty cents on the cash register.

She put the sack in Amy's hand and said, "That will be fifty cents, please."

Amy was confused for she hadn't meant to tell the clerk that she would buy it; she had only meant that she would like to buy it. Amy opened her hand which held the money from Mrs. Anchor. The clerk took the half dollar, put it in the cash register, and walked away.

Well, Amy thought, anyway I'll have a bracelet like the other girls. She left the store and snapped the bracelet on her wrist.

As Amy walked toward home, she thought how lovely the bracelet looked on her wrist and how nice it felt bouncing against her hand. But as she walked along, she began to wish that it had been banana charms dangling from the chain. And by the time she neared Jeannine's house, it began to feel heavy on her wrist, for she was thinking of Desert and Berne.

Jeannine ran out of her house when she saw Amy in front of her yard, and they met at the gate. "Oh, Amy," she exclaimed, "you bought it."

After the excitement of discovery was over, she examined the bracelet carefully. "Kick . . . that . . . ball . . . kick . . . that . . . ball," she read. "Oh, how funny." She went into a fit of giggles.

For the first time in their friendship, Jeannine's sense of humor surpassed Amy's. "I don't see anything the least bit funny," she told Jeannine crossly.

Jeannine draped herself over the fence and put both hands over her mouth, but the giggles still came through. As Amy turned and walked on, she could hear Jeannine gasping, "Kick that ball, kick that ball," between giggles. Amy felt the footballs growing heavier and heavier on her wrist and heard the gravel under her feet saying, "Kick that ball, kick that ball."

At home as Amy was putting her quarter in the money box, Berne came in. He saw Amy's slip of paper marked "twenty-five cents, housework," and he also saw the bracelet on her arm. He looked at Amy in rather an odd way, but he didn't say anything. He marked a slip of paper "thirty cents, rabbits for Mr.

Porter," put it and the money in the box and walked away. Amy wished he had asked about the bracelet, so she could explain that the clerk at Orson's had made a mistake.

For the rest of the afternoon whenever Berne saw her, he looked at her in the same odd way. She began to think of Desert and how he ran over the pasture with his light mane and tail flying and with his head held high. She began to think that even if they did have the fifty dollars by September first, she really didn't deserve to own a share in Desert, for Berne had earned most of the money. Now when she had earned a little, she had spent most of it on a silly charm bracelet.

Amy stayed with Jill while their mother went to Relief Society. Jill coaxed Amy to take her up the barnyard lane to look for ladybugs in the tall weeds by the fence. As Amy walked over the hard ground, her feet said, "Kick that ball, kick that ball." She unsnapped the bracelet from her wrist and put it in her pocket, but her feet said the same, "Kick that ball, kick that ball," all the way back to the house. Amy and Jill went into the living room to read *Amelia Anne Stiggins,* and Amy was very relieved to sit down, so her feet would be still.

They were reading the page of the book which told why Amelia's brothers and sisters were unable to go to the party when the telephone rang. It was Jeannine.

"Hello, Jeannine," Amy said a little on guard when Jill finally handed her the phone.

"Oh, Amy, was the bracelet you bought the last one—the very last one at Orson's?" Jeannine talked so fast that Amy had to listen carefully to understand her.

"Yes," Amy replied, feeling very disturbed that Jeannine had called to tease her about buying a bracelet with football charms.

"Oh, what ever shall I do?" Jeannine moaned. "I dropped my bracelet in the hay baler. I looked and looked, but all I found were a few pieces. It's ruined—ruined!"

"Maybe you could get another one in Cottonwood," Amy suggested, no longer angry when she found that Jeannine was sincere.

"I thought of that," Jeannine answered, "but Mother said we weren't going all the way to Cottonwood just for another bracelet. It will probably be weeks before we go to Cottonwood again. What ever shall I do?"

Then Amy had an idea—an idea which took the kick-that-ball out of her footsteps, an idea which made her unashamed to look Berne in the eye, an idea which made her heart sing as she finished reading *Amelia Anne* to Jill later.

"Would you like my bracelet?" she asked.

"Oh, Amy, would you sell it?"

When Amy assured her that she would, Jeannine began to rave about the beautiful football charm bracelet, and she was still raving ten minutes later when she reached Amy's house.

"Oh, thank you, Amy!" Jeannine sighed, and she

snapped the bracelet on her wrist before she stepped out of the door.

"You're welcome," Amy replied warmly with the fifty cents clutched in her hand. "You're very, very welcome."

As quickly as Amy had forgiven Jeannine, Berne forgave Amy when he learned the whole story.

Mrs. Anchor called Amy to work for her again that Friday and said she wanted her to come every Saturday as well. So Amy began regularly to put money in the box for Desert.

Chapter 7

As she always did, Amy felt a little anxious when the children neared the Peneck barn. Whenever she and Berne went to watch Desert, she hoped they wouldn't see Mr. Peneck. But they usually did. He had never been angry with them for coming but, just the same, he hadn't smiled very much either and his gruff voice made Amy feel very timid. Today Jill was with them too, and you never could tell what Jill would do.

"There he is!" Jill cried suddenly, running toward a black mare that was tied near the saddle room door.

"Oh, Jill," Berne scoffed, "that old Crowbait isn't Desert. Desert's a sorrel; that means red-red!"

Jill rejoined them sheepishly.

The moment they rounded the corner of the barn they saw Desert, with his head through the pasture fence, feeding on some choice grass that grew in the barnyard.

"There he is, Jill," Amy spoke reverently.

Jill ran at him so fast that Desert pulled his head back through the wires and trotted to the far side of the pasture.

"You frightened him away," Amy moaned.

"Jill," Berne informed her officially, "that is *not* how you walk up to a horse."

The children stepped to the barn doorway and waited there quietly for five minutes before Desert returned to the fence. Then, with Amy holding Jill's hand tightly and Berne talking softly, they walked slowly toward Desert. He watched them cautiously but stayed near the fence just out of reach.

"Isn't he beautiful," Amy breathed, as she placed her hand on the wire between two barbs.

"He's red," Jill announced as though she had just made a discovery, "but sort of orange. I colored you orange flavor." She pulled a crumpled paper from her pocket and noisily unfolded it. "See, Desert." She pushed the paper between the wires toward the horse. "It's a picture of you."

It was because of her funny orange scribbled paper that Jill had insisted on coming to Mr. Peneck's with Amy and Berne. Amy couldn't tell which side of the picture was up, but Jill had thought it very good and wanted to show it to Desert.

The sorrel raised and lowered his head slowly. Both Berne and Amy laughed to think that he understood about Jill's picture.

At that moment Mr. Peneck came around the barn leading the black mare.

"How's your horse today?" he asked.

"Fine, fine," Berne answered as Mr. Peneck put the mare in the pasture and closed the gate.

Suddenly Jill dashed toward the gate. "See," she beamed at Mr. Peneck. "See what I drew." She held her picture up in his face.

Amy held her breath, for surely, she thought, Mr. Peneck would be very annoyed.

Mr. Peneck slipped the bridle he was holding to his shoulder. He took Jill's picture and examined it carefully.

"That's very nice," he commented. "I believe it's a horse, isn't it?"

"It's Desert," Jill grinned.

"Yes, of course," Mr. Peneck patted Jill on the head as he handed back her picture.

Jill grabbed Mr. Peneck's hand and walked with him toward the barn. "What are you doing?" she asked.

"I'm going to gather the eggs." Mr. Peneck actually smiled.

"I'd like to help you," Jill suggested.

"Come along then," Mr. Peneck chuckled deeply.

Amy remembered herself then; she closed her mouth and tried not to stare after them.

When they returned from gathering eggs (with Jill only breaking one), Mr. Peneck remained with the children at the fence watching the horses. Amy glanced at him with wonder, but he didn't seem to notice.

"It won't be long now until Desert is yours," he encouraged them as they were leaving.

"Good-bye," Jill called, and waved as long as she could see him. "Mr. Peneck is my friend," she said when they were out on the road walking toward home.

"And Berne, he called our horse Desert," Amy mused.

"Of course," Berne said. "Desert is a much better name than Duncan and he knows it."

Amy was still feeling a little amazed when they turned the corner onto their street and caught up with Hurley Thick, who was walking on the roadside whacking weeds with a long stick.

"Hi, Hurley," Berne greeted.

Hurley stopped chopping and walked down the road with the Jackson children without pulling Jill's hair once.

"Ya don't know anyone who wants to hire a thirteen-year-old kid to do something or other, do ya?" Hurley was thirteen already. His birthday had been last week. Berne wouldn't be thirteen for several months yet. Hurley should have been in Berne's class at school, but he didn't do very well in school work and had been kept back a couple of years, so he was in Amy's class instead.

"Are you looking for a job?" Berne questioned.

"Yup," Hurley explained, "I can have Billy Jensen's paper route when he quits if I have a bike by then."

"I just don't know, Hurley," Berne admitted. "I just don't know where you could get work. Jobs are hard to find in Jacksonville."

"How much does a bike cost?" asked Amy.

"About forty dollars," Hurley growled without even adding Amy Pamy. "And I've just earned five dollars and twelve cents." He dropped the stick and let his hands hang limply at his side, the ragged cuffs of his shirt way above his wrists.

"Well, that's a good start," said Amy encouragingly.

But she wondered how he would ever be able to earn the other thirty-five dollars in just two weeks. She and Berne had only forty-one dollars and four cents, and they had been working all summer for that. They still had three weeks to earn the remaining nine dollars. But if Dad hadn't made the bargain to give them as much as they earned, they would never be able to get Desert. But Hurley didn't have a Dad to help him out. Amy wanted to suggest that maybe he could eat some worms for five dollars apiece as he had done once before. It would only take seven worms to make thirty-five dollars, but Hurley left them and walked to his yard.

"I'll let you know if I hear of anything," called Berne, as Hurley scuffed at a clod of dirt near his gate.

"I hope he can earn enough money," Amy commented as they continued on. "I think he wants the paper route badly."

"I hope so too," Berne replied, "but there's not much chance."

As they entered their yard, Amy was struck with the prospect of doing nothing the rest of the afternoon. "Let's do something," she suggested hopefully. "Maybe we could walk down to Clear Creek and do something that's fun."

"Oh boy!" said Jill, "we could catch bugs and spiders."

"Nope," Berne said, "I'm going rabbit hunting."

Amy waited for Berne to say "Do you want to come along?" but he didn't, so she finally asked, "Can we go too?"

"Nope, girls are sissies. They cry too much." Berne had never forgotten the day they had gone to the oaks.

"But, Berne," began Amy, "we won't . . ."

"I want to go rabbit hunting," Jill insisted.

"Nope," said Berne. He went into the house and returned with his pump gun.

"Please, please, please," coaxed Jill, but Berne turned away. "Please, please, please," she shouted after him.

The farther he walked, the louder she shouted. But Berne didn't even look around. He just kept going as if he didn't hear Jill. Amy wished she could ignore Jill like Berne did, especially when Jill was pleading,

"Please, please, please." Amy could hear her quite well and usually ended up giving in.

Jill shouted, "Please, please, please," for quite awhile, until she was sure Berne was too far away to hear.

Amy wished Berne had taken them with him, because it would be such a long afternoon just sitting on the back porch longing for Desert.

Jill took her picture of Desert from her pocket, but she couldn't remember which side was up and which was down. One way it looked like a haystack and the other way it looked like a rabbit with four ears.

"Amy," said Jill, "let's go rabbit hunting!"

"Amy," said Jill, getting more excited at the thought, "let's go rabbit hunting *ourselves!*"

Why not? Yes, of course we could, thought Amy; we don't need Berne.

"Okay."

"I'll get my gun!" Jill rushed into the house, banging the screen door after her. In a moment she returned with her toy pistol.

"We could go rabbit hunting down by Clear Creek," suggested Amy. "There are lots of rabbits out that way." She was really thinking how pleasant it was to play by Clear Creek. "But we'll need a sack to hunt rabbits with. Toy guns don't work so well." In a sack they could collect moss, mint and joint grass.

"Oh boy!" exclaimed Jill.

She had never been rabbit hunting like this. She laid her toy gun on the porch railing.

"Let's find Dad," said Amy, starting toward the barn.

"Oh boy!" Jill repeated, running to catch up with her.

They found their father behind the barn unloading rocks from the pickup.

"Dad," asked Amy, "may we borrow a gunny sack?"

"Why do you want a gunny sack?" he asked, as he lifted a geode from the truck.

"We're going rabbit hunting!" said Jill excitedly.

Dad was even more puzzled. "Why do you want a gunny sack to go rabbit hunting?"

Amy felt a little foolish.

"To catch rabbits with!" explained Jill as though that were the usual way to go rabbit hunting.

He shrugged his shoulders. "Oh, well, in *that* case, there's one here in the pickup you can use."

After Amy got the gunny sack out of the pickup, she and Jill ducked under the barbed wire fence into the alfalfa field to take the shortest way to Clear Creek. They walked along the bank of the irrigation ditch that cut through the middle of the field so they wouldn't tromp down the tall alfalfa, for their father couldn't mow it if it were lying flat on the ground.

The irrigation ditch was empty now and completely dry, but where the water had been the ground was wrinkled and broken into thousands of mud cracks. The sisters sat down in the ditch to peel up the cracked mud. Amy tried to get a whole section up without breaking it. Jill looked carefully underneath each to find crawling creatures that might be there. She found several ants and a small worm.

"We'll have to go on," said Amy finally, "if we're going to have enough time for rabbit hunting."

She picked up the gunny sack again and started off. Jill followed with sections of cracked mud in her hands.

"Why are you bringing those pieces of dirt?" Amy asked her.

"Because they're such pretty shapes," Jill explained. "This one looks like Mr. Peneck, and this one looks like Desert, and this one looks like a rabbit."

Jill carried the dirt for awhile, but it was too hard to catch grasshoppers with her hands full of dirt, so she put the pieces in her blouse pocket. They crumbled, however, when she crawled under the fence that separated the alfalfa field from the pasture where Clear Creek ran.

"I don't see any rabbits," Jill observed.

"We'll wait for them," said Amy, "down by the creek."

Willows grew thick around the creek. As the sisters worked their way through the dense growth to the water, Amy broke off a small branch and put it in the sack.

"Why are you putting sticks in our rabbit sack?" Jill asked.

"So Dad can make me a willow whistle when we get home," Amy answered.

"Oh," said Jill. She broke off a switch and dropped it into the sack. Then she took the dirt from her pocket and dumped it in the sack too. It wasn't long until the gunny sack was heavy with mint, moss, water spiders, and sparkling stones from the stream. The girls caught some polliwogs but decided to let them go.

The water looked inviting, so the girls removed their shoes, dangled their bare feet into the cool water, and talked.

"We almost have enough money to buy Desert," Amy told Jill, "and tomorrow we will have even more, for I'm going to help Mrs. Anchor again."

"Maybe I'll have another nickel," volunteered Jill. Last week she had contributed a nickel which Mother had given her for an ice cream cone for Desert. Jill loved ice cream, so it had been a hard sacrifice.

"That would be very nice."

"Or maybe I'll give it to Hurley," said Jill, "for his bike."

"I think that would be fine," replied Amy.

"I'll be able to ride Desert, won't I?"

"Of course. Dad said he would break him right away." Amy looked out through the willows at the pasture, and it was easy to imagine Desert galloping across it with her on his back.

The girls pulled their feet from the cold water and wiped them on the grass. After they put on their shoes, they walked to a patch of joint grass and began gathering handfuls to stuff in the sack.

Softly, as though from a great distance, the girls heard, "Wooooooo—, wooo, wooo, woooooooooooo—." They both stopped and looked up toward the sound. The sun had gone down and the whole pasture looked gray in the dim light of dusk. It was later than they had realized.

"We'd better go home," Amy suggested.

"Wooooooo—, wooo, wooo, woooooooooooo—," came the sound again.

"What's that?" asked Jill nervously.

"It sounds like a howling coyote to me," said Amy.

"Maybe it's a goblin," said Jill, hoping as she looked behind her, that it was a coyote instead.

Amy picked up the sack, and she and Jill walked quickly around a big hollow log toward the pasture fence. Suddenly a gray shadow streaked from under a bush and disappeared into the log.

"A goblin!!" cried Jill, frozen in her tracks.

"It's a rabbit!!" sputtered Amy, jumping up and down.

"A rabbit!" squealed Jill, forgetting all about the goblins.

She ran to the hollow where the shadow had disappeared and stretched her arm as far into the log as she could. But she felt nothing except the rotted wood.

"Don't move," Amy ordered. "Stay right there and be quiet!"

Amy ran around to the other end of the log. She sat down in front of it and put her back over the opening. Quickly she turned the gunny sack upside down and shook the rocks, moss, sticks, spiders, and grass on the ground.

"What are you doing?" whispered Jill from the other end of the log.

"Be quiet," said Amy. Jill could whisper so loud. Amy carefully fitted the gunny sack over the end of the log. "Now make lots of noise, Jill. Bang around inside the log with your hands and some sticks."

Making noise was Jill's specialty and she did a grand job. She shouted into the log, "Where are you, rabbit? Here, bunny bunny." She hit the inside of the log with a stick, and she kicked the ground. Then she made squealing noises that would have frightened the master goblin himself.

The poor rabbit completely lost its wits and dashed toward the opposite end of the log. He was going pretty fast when he hit the bottom of the gunny sack and tumbled head over heels. Amy quickly pulled the sack off the log and gathered the top together.

Jill, at the other end of the log, was still shrieking her head off.

"We caught him; we caught him," cried Amy. "We caught our rabbit!"

Jill stopped shrieking shrieks and instead began yipping yips. She ran to Amy and felt the burlap with its soft, warm lump. Amy twisted the top of the sack tightly, then grasped the bottom in such a way that the rabbit was nestled in her arms.

"He's shaking," she said. "Poor thing," and she held him close, petted him through the sack and talked softly to him. "Nice little bunny, nice little bunny. Were you frightened?"

Jill danced around her singing, "A rabbit! a rabbit! We caught a rabbit!"

The girls walked across the pasture and climbed through the fence. By now it was almost dark. As they walked along the ditch bank, they heard far away, "Wooooooo—, wooo, wooo, wooooooooooo."

Jill walked faster. "There's a goblin howling in my head," she complained.

"It's a dog or a coyote," Amy supposed.

But Jill kept looking behind her. No goblin was going to get her because she didn't watch out. But as soon as they climbed through the fence into the barnyard, Jill felt better because she could hear Berne whistling "The Old Chisholm Trail."

The girls ran to the house. Berne, their father, and the animal doctor were standing on the back porch.

"Here they are," Dad called.

Mother came out from the kitchen. "Where in the world have you girls been?"

"Rabbit hunting," said Jill.

The girls ran onto the porch and Amy sat down in the path of light shining through the screen door.

"How many rabbits did you catch?" asked Dad.

"Only one," replied Amy.

She laid the sack in her lap, carefully holding the top edges together.

"Goodness," said Mother, "there *is* something in that sack."

"It's a rabbit," Jill sang out, and she jumped up

and down chanting, "A rabbit, a rabbit, we caught a rabbit."

"Well, I'll be . . ." exclaimed the animal doctor.

"Let's see," said Dad.

He put his hand into the bag, and felt around for a moment. Then he pulled a very small gray rabbit out by the neck. Too frightened to struggle, it hung limply from Dad's hand.

"Oh, he looks so lonesome and frightened." Amy took him in her arms. He wiggled his head down under her arm trying to hide from everyone.

"I'll name him Evening," Amy decided, "because that's when we caught him and because he is sort of that color." For the moment Amy forgot all about Desert.

"Goodness!" There seemed nothing else Mother could say.

Berne stroked the rabbit's back with one finger. "How did you ever . . . ?" he asked.

He could hardly believe it. He had been rabbit hunting all afternoon without seeing one. He wished he had gone with Amy and Jill instead of by himself.

The animal doctor chuckled, "These girls are just what I need. They would be better than box traps to catch prairie dogs—and skunks too."

"Where can we put him?" asked Amy.

"Well, I don't know . . ." said Mother, wondering whether she should let them keep him.

"I'll fix a pen," Berne took over. "I know just what will be good." He dashed off toward the barn.

"Well," Mother looked at Dad.

"He's a cute little cottontail," Dad remarked.

"I suppose it's all right," said Mother.

Berne soon returned with an orange crate and some boards. "This will do for tonight. Early in the morning I'll make him a real pen."

While he was arranging the temporary enclosure on the back porch, Jill ran to the barn for some straw. She put it inside the crate. "For a bed," she said. Dad brought some fresh alfalfa leaves for Evening to eat, and Mother found an old jar lid and filled it with water for him to drink. Amy laid him carefully in the box, and the animal doctor put boards on the top, with rocks to weight them. Evening crouched in the back of the pen and stared out at them.

"All right," Mother ordered, "come in the house and get washed up for supper."

As they all walked in to supper, Jill sang loudly, "A rabbit, a rabbit, we caught a rabbit. A rabbit, a rabbit, we caught a rabbit."

For half a week Amy fed Evening three times a day, cleaned his pen carefully, and even carried him about with her. But gradually she began coming to his pen less regularly, and by the end of the week she saw him only when she fed him once a day.

When she wasn't working to earn money, she spent her time by Mr. Peneck's fence, in the barn that would be Desert's home, or in Berne's room counting the money in the box. Gathering alfalfa leaves for Evening became a chore. Perhaps it was because Evening wasn't adventurous, not even as adventurous as Vacuum. And Evening gave Amy nothing to think about. Perhaps it was because Great-grandfather had not had a wondrous gray rabbit named Evening, but a wondrous sorrel horse named Desert. Plain and simple, Evening, Amy's wild rabbit, was a bother.

One morning after breakfast, Mother called Amy out on the back porch. "You didn't feed and water your rabbit yesterday," she said, pointing to Evening in his makeshift pen. "And Berne never did make a good pen for him."

"I'll feed him right now," Amy repented, but she stood looking at Evening for a moment. Suddenly the rabbit stuck its nose between the slates and wrinkled it at her. It was plain enough to Amy; she wrinkled her nose back at him.

"I think it would be a good plan," said Mother, choosing her words carefully, "to take him back to the pasture and turn him loose."

She watched Amy, expecting a defensive outburst.

"I think it would be a good plan too," Amy agreed. "Wild rabbits should be wild."

Mother was more than a little surprised, but she said quietly, "Take him to the pasture before Jill finishes snacking on leftover toast crusts. For she will surely kick up a fuss about it. I will have Berne take the crate back to the barn right away."

Amy hurried through the barnyard and alfalfa field with the rabbit held tightly in one arm. The rabbit didn't wiggle until she put him between the wires of the pasture fence. Then he streaked off, rippling the tall grass all the way to Clear Creek.

"Wild rabbits should be wild," Amy repeated to herself as she turned back toward the barnyard.

When she reached the house, Jill was sitting where the crate had been with a paper and pencil drawing a picture of some creature with five long legs and one long neck. "Let's go over to Mr. Peneck's this morning," she coaxed. "Let's go over and watch Desert."

And Jill never once asked about Evening, the wild rabbit.

Chapter 8

"Amy, I'm ready to study skunks today," the animal doctor greeted her as she sat down to her bowl of breakfast cereal.

"Do skunks get sick like prairie dogs?" Amy asked as she poured some cream on her cereal.

"I suppose so." Dr. Heeps' eyes twinkled merrily, "but I'm only concerned about the healthy ones—what they eat, where they live, and what they do."

"Do you want an egg, Amy?" Mother was cutting hard-boiled eggs into a bowl of potato salad.

"No, thanks," Amy replied.

The animal doctor leaned back on his chair and smiled. "I'll bet Amy would like to go to the mountains today, too."

"Yes, I would," Amy quickly affirmed.

"More lunch, Mrs. Jackson," the animal doctor joked.

"Are we going to watch skunks eat?" Amy asked.

"I wish we could, but we'll only be trying to locate them today. Berne's going to show me where he and your dad saw some recently. Your father couldn't go because he had to take a load of rocks to Cottonwood."

"The lunch is almost ready," said Mother, "then you can be on your way."

As Amy gulped her cereal to finish it, Berne strode in the back door.

"Dad has left," he informed them. "Say, Dr. Heeps, we've got more than enough money to buy Desert; that is with the money I'll earn mowing lawns tomorrow."

The animal doctor joggled on his chair as though he were riding a horse. "Desert of the red sands," he teased.

"Let's go." The animal doctor held the screen door open for Berne and Amy, and Mother handed Berne the lunch box.

"I want to go too," insisted Jill, who left the porch and followed closely behind Berne sniffing at the lunch box. "Mother, can I go too? Please, please, please."

"No, dear, you'd only be in the way."

"Oh, let her go," Dr. Heeps urged. "We'll be back before dark. She won't be in the way."

"All right," Mother relented, "but Jill, you do just what Dr. Heeps says."

Berne put the lunch box in the back of the truck. The animal doctor picked up some wooden stakes from the ground nearby. Just as he stepped on the running board to put them in the pickup, Hurley and Winston Thick ambled out of the orchard toward them.

"Amy Pamy is a damy." Hurley scuffed up to Amy and jerked her hair.

"Hi, Hurley," greeted the animal doctor as he slid behind the steering wheel.

"Howdy," Hurley replied, stomping up and down where he was standing.

"Hello, Winston," said the animal doctor.

Winston silently peered at the animal doctor from under his thick, curly hair.

"Isn't it the day after tomorrow that Billy Jensen is quitting and you will get his paper route," Berne asked Hurley. "How are you coming on your bike money?"

"I don't want that old paper route anyway," stated Hurley gruffly. "I'm going to buy a football and lots of other things with the fifteen dollars I've earned." He stomped up and down so hard that he stepped on Winston's toe as Winston crowded near him to peek in the pickup at the animal doctor.

Hurley looked so downcast that the animal doctor said, "Hurley, why don't you and Winston come with us? We're going into the mountains to look for spotted skunks. We'll be back before dark."

Hurley brightened a little at this. He climbed in the cab of the truck, and Winston jumped in beside him. They didn't have to ask their mother if they could go, for she worked all day and wouldn't be home until late.

"Amy and I will ride in the back," volunteered Berne, climbing over the rear fender. Amy followed him.

"I will too," said Jill, who had been leaning over the side of the pickup examining the lunch box.

"Okay," said the animal doctor, "we'll take turns riding in the front."

Everyone settled down for the ride as the pickup pulled slowly out of the driveway. The pickup sped through town and up the canyon. As it turned onto a dirt road, clouds of dust billowed up from the rear and powdered the scrub oaks and elderberry bushes that grew near.

Jill was sitting in the corner of the pickup bed near the lunch box. The longer she sat there, the more distinctly she smelled delicious aromas creeping out from between the flaps. Something smelled like apples, and she wondered what it would be. Finally she decided she would peek in to see whether it was apple pie or applesauce cake.

She lifted the top flap a little and put her eyes to the crack, but she could see only darkness. However, she could smell apple something a lot better. She tried to raise the flaps higher, but Mother had interlaid them so that Jill couldn't budge them. She braced both feet against the bottom of the box and pulled with all her strength. The flaps popped open just as Jill toppled backwards, landing in the animal doctor's wooden stakes and pulling the lunch box on top of her. The stakes began rattling around, almost bouncing out of the pickup.

Amy and Berne jumped up and began rapidly gathering them up.

"It's apple pie," said Jill, lifting it off her chest and holding it to her mouth to nibble on the edge of the crust.

"Jill, stop that and put it back in the box," Amy ordered as she tipped the lunch box upright and rearranged the contents with her one hand that wasn't full of stakes.

But Jill kept nibbling.

"Stop that." As Amy grabbed the pie from Jill, a stake dropped from her arms into it, making a big hole in the center. Jill picked up the stake and licked off the juicy apples.

Berne closed the lunch box and piled up the animal doctor's stakes again. "Okay, Jill, move!" And he made her sit down in the opposite corner.

They had been climbing sharply and now were in the pine and fir forest where the road was less steep. The pickup gathered speed, bouncing the children around on the dusty bed, and the wind blew their hair into twisted mats on their heads.

They passed a steep embankment on which wild raspberry bushes grew. Berne tapped on the back window of the cab. The animal doctor slowed down and stopped. Hurley climbed into the back and Berne got in the front with the animal doctor to show him the way.

They left the dirt road and followed a track that was barely visible through the tall mountain grass. It wound in and out among the trees, over knolls and down through little gullies. Even though they went very slowly, it was the bumpiest part of the ride.

Hurley sat to one side, bouncing up and down every time they hit a bump. He made no effort to hang on to the side of the pickup to keep from bouncing. Amy wondered if he were thinking about the paper route, and she wished he had been able to earn the money. She knew he really wanted the job—probably as much as she and Berne wanted Desert.

Most people didn't like Hurley very much, for he usually stomped around, pushed people, and said silly things. But he wasn't really as bad as everyone said, Amy thought, for he didn't do mean things like some of the big junior high school boys in Cottonwood. Even the kids at school didn't like Hurley very well. They thought he was dumb because he had been held back two years. And even though he had been required to take two grades twice, he still didn't do very well with his school work.

Amy remembered once Miss Applegate had called on Hurley to read. It was a rather difficult book to read, but Hurley managed to stumble along until he came to the word, "conventionally," which he read "contented." It *had* sounded funny in the sentence, and everyone in the class had laughed. Hurley grunted and sat down without reading another word. Amy couldn't remember if she had laughed with the class. She hoped not.

The pickup slowed and stopped in a small clearing surrounded by tall ponderosa pines. The girls stood up to stretch. It felt good not to be bounced around anymore.

"We're going to walk into the forest," said the animal doctor as he and Berne got out of the cab, "so Berne can show me where he and his dad saw the spotted skunks. We'll only be gone a short time. The rest of you stay close to the truck. And for Pete's sake, don't wander away."

All the children piled out of the pickup. Amy sat down on a rock and watched a red-shafted flicker in a dead tree close to her.

Jill found a tiny stream that trickled just at the edge of the clearing. She started scouring it for salamanders, but was satisfied when she caught a water spider and a fly. Winston followed close behind her, all set to pounce on whatever she found and claim it for his own.

Hurley occupied himself throwing pine cones at the trunk of a large ponderosa pine. When a squirrel began chattering from high among the branches, he threw cones at it. The squirrel scolded loudly at him, then with its tail jerking back and forth scampered higher into the tree. Hurley kept peppering the tree with cones, but now the squirrel was much too high to hit.

For awhile Amy enjoyed sitting and watching the bird. But suddenly the flicker flew away in a flurry of white and orange flashes, and Amy began to wish the animal doctor and Berne would come back. Finally, for want of something better to do, Amy joined Jill and Winston at the tiny stream.

The children slowly wandered downstream. They found a pile of decaying timber and stopped to watch ants crawl busily through it. A little farther they ran onto a tiny waterfall and amused themselves by floating sticks over it. As they walked on toward a patch of lupine, Amy realized they had moved out of sight of the pickup, but she decided it would be easy to find the way back by just returning upstream.

Suddenly Jill saw a horny toad streak across a heap of dried, decayed pine cones under a ponderosa. She took up the chase, but the horny toad scuttled off into a jumble of logs. Winston and Amy ran to help her, but Jill already had caught it.

"My, it's pretty, Jill," said Amy. "I've never seen one tinged with orange before. The toads I've found have been plain gray or tan."

"I want one too." Winston looked longingly at Jill's hand, but she had a good hold on the toad. As he glanced around to see if another one was near, he glimpsed something moving among the trees. "Look!" he sputtered, pointing vigorously into the forest.

Both Amy and Jill became quite as excited as Winston, for there, walking unconcernedly into a patch of aspen seedlings, was a spotted skunk.

"We had better see where it goes so we can tell the animal doctor," whispered Amy as she tiptoed toward the skunk.

Jill and Winston walked cautiously after her. The skunk continued through the aspens and meandered across a clearing. The children followed as quietly as they could. The skunk ambled through the forest for almost half an hour with the children tracking it at a safe distance. Finally it disappeared into a thick patch of gooseberry bushes, dwarf pines, and fallen logs. Though the children walked around the patch several times, they saw nothing more of the animal.

"That's where it lives." Amy took off one of her pink socks and tied it to a pine that stood nearby. "Now we can find the place when we come back to show the animal doctor. Let's go and get him."

She turned back into the forest. But Jill walked in a different direction.

"Where are you going?" Amy asked her.

"Back to the pickup."

"It's this way."

"No, it's this way," Jill argued.

Amy looked at the towering trees on every side, and suddenly she realized that she didn't know where they were.

"Are you sure it's that way?" she hopefully questioned Jill.

"Well, maybe it is," Jill answered.

"It's that way." Winston pointed in a third direction.

It was then that Amy remembered the size of the mountain and the forest. It was then that she remembered hearing Dad say you could walk for days in the forest without finding roads or people or an end to the tall ponderosa pines. It was then that she remembered the animal doctor telling them very plainly, "For Pete's sake, don't wander away."

"We'll have to be careful not to get lost," Amy explained, not willing to admit to Jill and Winston that they were already lost. "We'll walk a little way in each direction, but not out of sight of my stocking. Then we might remember which way we came."

In a few minutes they were back at the ponderosa and the pink stocking, still just as puzzled as to where they were.

"We'll stay here," Amy planned. "Dad said never to wander around if you don't know where you're going; he says that's a sure way to get lost. So we'll stay here until someone finds us."

Jill put her horny toad on the ground and then caught it when it began to streak away. Winston pulled pine cones apart. *They* certainly didn't seem worried about being lost in the forest. But Amy was, and every once in a while she would make Winston and Jill shout with her for help just as loud as they could. Amy hoped the animal doctor would hear them and come to them. But nothing happened.

"I'm hungry," Jill complained after they had waited for awhile, "awful hungry."

"Me, too," Winston agreed.

"I want to go back to the pickup and eat right now," demanded Jill. "Let's go."

"No!" said Amy decidedly, "we have to wait right here. Let's shout again."

"I'm still hungry," insisted Jill after they called. "And I still want to go."

"We have to wait." Amy thought fast. "But I'll tell you a story."

The story Amy told was about Great-grandfather's Desert and the time that Nancy was lost. Nancy was Great-grandfather's youngest daughter and young Arthur's little sister. She was only about three years old when the family went northeast from the ranch to the foothills to pick chokecherries. They found some trees weighed down with them and picked all they wanted. As they loaded into the wagon, Nancy joined them, her face and dress smeared with dark purple berry juice.

But it wasn't chokecherry juice. For chokecherries aren't that good; they make very good jelly, but they taste bitter when eaten plain.

Great-grandmother threw up her hands. "What have you been eating?"

In reply Nancy showed the family some bushes in a nearby gully. Great-grandmother was relieved to find they were wild currants and nothing poisonous. They picked all of the sweet, fat berries, eating most of them, but saving a few to take home for pies. Nancy loved the currants and ate them from Great-grandmother's dishpan as they rode back to the farm in the wagon.

When they reached home, Great-grandmother made the currant pies, and as they were baking, Nancy came in.

"I want some more currants," she said, looking in the dish pan.

"They're all in the pies, Nancy," Great-grandmother replied.

"I'll just have to pick some more then."

"Yes, we will have to do that one of these days." And Great-grandmother went on busily with the housework.

"I sure would like some currant pie," Jill interrupted, "or some apple pie."

"If you go walking off to get some now," Amy warned her, "the same thing will happen to you that happened to Nancy."

"What happened to Nancy?" Winston glanced anxiously at the rows of silent trees.

"Nancy got lost, that's what," Amy replied.

Much later at supper time the family discovered Nancy was missing, Amy continued the story. They ate their meal believing she would surely come walking in with a handful of wild flowers picked from along the wagon trail or with hay clinging to her hair from playing on the stack. But after supper when she hadn't returned, the family began to look for her.

They looked on the trail and by the haystack, then they searched the whole farm carefully. Finally Great-grandmother recalled Nancy saying she would have to pick some more currants. Perhaps she had gone back to the foothills.

It was dark by the time Great-grandfather had saddled up Desert and started after Nancy. But when he reached the place where they had picked berries, the moon was up to light his way. Though he searched long, he couldn't find her, and though he called loud, he couldn't hear an answer.

Giving up, he turned Desert homeward, but the horse refused to go and looked nervously toward the foothills. So Great-grandfather loosened the reins, and Desert picked his way uneasily over a knoll and down into a gully. From somewhere in the undergrowth near the top of the gully, Great-grandfather heard the scream of a bobcat.

Suddenly the animal streaked out of the undergrowth and disappeared over a hill. Desert continued up the gully near the undergrowth where the bobcat had been hiding. On the ground was a small heap, which looked very much like a little girl. Great-grandfather quickly swung off Desert. There was Nancy, curled up asleep in the soft earth of the gully side. Beside her, neatly folded, was her dress, which she had taken off before going to bed in the dirt.

Great-grandfather picked her up gently and took her home. She remained asleep during the entire journey to the ranch. That was the kind of sleeper Nancy was. And Desert had found her and saved her from the bobcat. That was the kind of horse Desert was.

"Now we'd better shout again," said Amy when she finished the story.

"I wish we had Desert now! He'd find us." Jill's voice was hoarse from shouting so much.

"Are there really bobcats in these mountains?" Winston looked around uneasily.

"Oh, yes," Amy informed him, "lots of them."

Winston gulped and began picking pine cones apart much faster than before. "Are there mountain lions here too?"

"Oh yes, lots of mountain lions live here too."

Then Winston stopped picking at the cones and, listening intently, stared into the forest.

Amy heard the noise too, a crackling of dried branches.

"Is it a mountain lion?" breathed Winston.

"I don't think so," Amy whispered. "I don't think they make that much noise. They have soft feet. They sneak up on you silently from behind."

Winston glanced hurriedly and nervously behind himself.

The slight crackling of dead branches which they had heard now increased to a loud noise accompanied by a swishing of the undergrowth. Suddenly out from a thick patch of aspens stepped Hurley.

"Hurley!" shouted Winston, and he ran to him after looking behind himself just once more.

"Oh, Hurley! We are glad to see you," Amy sighed with relief. "We got lost following a spotted skunk."

"Let's go back to the truck then," said Hurley.

Jill picked the horny toad from her blouse where it had been clinging with its tiny sharp toes and followed quickly after the other children. "I'm hungry," she complained all the way back to the pickup.

The animal doctor and Berne were standing in the clearing when the four children walked up the little stream bank.

"Where in the world have you been?" asked the animal doctor. He and Berne had returned to the pickup some time ago. They had called and looked around and had been extremely worried when they could find no one.

"We followed a skunk and got lost," Amy explained. "Hurley came to look for us when we didn't come back and he finally heard us shouting and found us."

"I'm hungry," Jill informed everyone.

"Good work, Hurley," praised the animal doctor.

"Wasn't nothin'," said Hurley.

"I'm hungry." This time everyone heard Jill.

"Then let's eat." The animal doctor lifted the lunch box out of the pickup and began setting the contents on the grass. Luckily Mrs. Jackson had made a very large lunch, so there was plenty even with Hurley and Winston sharing the food.

"This is better than *Amelia Anne Stiggins*," Jill remarked as she helped herself.

Everyone had sandwiches, carrot sticks, salad, and the apple pie with a dented center and a nibbled crust.

"All right, Amy, let's see what you found." Dr. Heeps said, as he was putting the empty dishes into the truck and lifting out his stakes. "You lead the way."

"I don't think Amy knows a skunk from a badger," Berne scoffed, a little annoyed because the animal doctor had found no sign of skunks where he had taken him.

"Yes, I do," Amy contradicted. "It was a skunk we saw." Amy couldn't help strutting as she marched through the forest with everyone following her.

"It hid in those bushes," Amy informed the animal doctor as they reached the tree with the pink stocking.

"Great day in the morning!" exclaimed the animal doctor after he examined the ground. "This is tremendous! Here, Berne and Hurley, help me stake this area out to study." The animal doctor stepped off fifteen paces.

The boys began pounding stakes in the ground where Dr. Heeps indicated. Amy felt so successful that she wanted to help too; she tried hammering in one stake, but it just lay down flat instead of going into the soil. By the third attempt, Hurley walked up and said, "Ha, Amy Pamy, you ain't going to get the stick in the ground by spanking it. Ha, ha." He took the stake and pounded it right in with three swings of the axe he was using.

Then, leaving Amy sitting on the ground feeling useless, Hurley went a little further to drive in the next marker. To clear a spot, he pushed aside some rocks, which tumbled down a small hill and crashed into a bush at the bottom. As Hurley bent over to pick up the stake, from under the bush swarmed a mass of yellow jackets. The cloud of insects descended on Hurley,

who ran away, grabbing handful after handful of dirt which he frantically threw over himself.

"Hurley!" Amy screamed. She ran toward him, not even thinking what she would do when she got there.

Before anyone could reach him, the swarm of yellow jackets and the cloud of dirt, with which Hurley was covering himself, separated from each other. The yellow jackets disappeared downhill, and the dirt settled slowly on Hurley, who crawled stunned along the ground.

"Hurley!" Amy cried again as she reached him.

"Are you all right?" The animal doctor came running up.

Hurley didn't answer, but just sat on the ground

looking a little like a gray statue. Dr. Heeps examined the stings which covered Hurley. Hurley began to swell—his face and hands, his arms and even shoulders, legs, and ankles where the bees had stung through his clothes.

"We'd better get you back to the pickup. Berne, you take one arm and I'll take the other," said the animal doctor.

"Naw," said Hurley "it ain't nothin'."

He pulled away from Dr. Heeps and Berne and walked by himself. The animal doctor followed closely behind and Berne carried the remaining stakes.

By the time they reached the pickup, Hurley looked puffy all over. The children piled into the back of the truck, but the animal doctor made Hurley lie down in the cab. All the time Hurley insisted, "Naw, it ain't nothin'."

The animal doctor drove pretty fast down the mountain and back to Jacksonville. It was a bumpy ride for the four in the back of the pickup, but Amy didn't mind a bit. She just held on tight to the side, thinking of Hurley's swollen, funny-colored face.

When they arrived in Jacksonville, the animal doctor pulled up in front of Dr. Applegate's house and took Hurley inside. He was still saying, "Naw, it ain't nothin'."

"It's sure too bad," Amy told Berne while they were waiting.

"Yes," agreed Berne. "Some people have all the bad luck."

"I wish he had enough money for a bike so he could have the paper route," Amy sighed.

"Yes, I do too," Berne replied. "I do too."

Finally the animal doctor and Hurley came back to the truck. Dr. Applegate had given Hurley a shot and some lotion to rub on the yellow-jacket stings. The animal doctor drove Hurley straight to his house and made him lie down. When Amy told her mother what had happened, she went to the Thick's and stayed there until Hurley's mother came home.

After supper was over and Amy was through helping with the dishes, she walked out on the back porch where she sat down on the steps. She remained alone in the dark thinking about Desert and the money she and Berne had earned and about Hurley and the money he couldn't earn. She thought about Great-grandfather's Desert and about Hurley's bee stings. The longer she thought, the sadder she became. By the time Berne came out on the porch and sat beside her, she was *very* sad. They watched the stars in silence for awhile.

Then Berne said, "Mother said we'd better go to bed pretty soon." His voice sounded sad too.

"Berne," said Amy cautiously, "I've been thinking."

"Oh." Berne was cautious himself.

"I've been thinking how lucky we are."

Berne didn't say aything.

"We've got Dad, and we've got bikes. We've got friends, and we've got money. And we've got Great-grandfather Jackson and all the stories about him and

Desert. Some people don't have anything we have. They don't have Dads, nor bikes, nor money, and they don't have great-grandfathers or Deserts that did anything special. They don't have friends, and people just laugh at them."

Berne nodded in the dark. He knew just which "some people" Amy meant.

Then Amy spoke very quietly, "Do you think we could help Hurley get his bike?"

For a moment Berne didn't answer. He was figuring. Hurley needed twenty-five more dollars by the day after tomorrow. They didn't need their fifty dollars for a week and two days, but twenty-five dollars would be difficult to earn by then. If they gave Hurley twenty-five dollars, they couldn't be sure of getting that much in such a short time.

"We could, but then we might not be able to get Desert."

"I know."

Both Berne and Amy thought of Desert running over Mr. Peneck's meadow with his light mane and tail streaming behind him in striking contrast to his beautiful sorrel hide. They thought of the way he held his head high and stomped his forefoot when he was impatient. And they thought of how much they wanted him.

"We have Great-grandfather's Desert." Amy swallowed a lump in her throat.

Berne stood up and walked to the kitchen door. He opened the screen door but stopped as he entered the doorway. A dozen moths flew in the house while he stood there silhouetted by the light from the kitchen.

Finally he said, "I'll take twenty-five dollars over to Hurley in the morning."

He stepped into the house and closed the screen behind him.

Chapter 9

Before breakfast on the thirtieth of August, Berne and Amy again counted the money in the box.

"Are you sure, Berne?" Amy asked.

"Sure, I'm sure."

"But we've worked so hard this week."

"Just thirty-three dollars and fifty-six cents," Berne insisted. "And with Dad's thirty-three fifty-six, that only makes sixty-seven dollars and twelve cents."

They solemnly joined the family for breakfast. No one seemed to notice how downcast they were, and the animal doctor said merrily, "Amy, I saw a new skunk yesterday not far from the place you discovered. You really hit the jackpot when you followed that skunk!"

"That's good." Amy smiled weakly.

"It looks like rain today," Mother said.

"Yes, I'll probably get wet, but come what may, I'm going to pace off that new area today and stake it out for study."

"Be careful and don't drive a stake through a yellow jacket nest," Dad joked.

"How is the Thick boy now?" asked the animal doctor.

"Fine," Mother answered. "He started his paper route just a couple of days after he was stung. He was still pretty lumpy looking then, but the swelling has gone down now."

Amy had seen Hurley ride past just yesterday as he was delivering papers. He sped up on his new red bike, took a rolled-up newspaper and threw it neatly onto the front porch. "Hi, Amy," he called jovially as he swung his bike around to go back up the street.

Both the animal doctor and Dad left the table in a hurry to be about their business. As Berne went out the back door, announcing that he was going rabbit hunting, Amy wanted to reassure him that she would think of something—some way that they could get their needed money. But she was afraid that her voice would tremble and that the tears, pushing pretty hard to get out, would come spilling down her cheeks.

Amy began to clear off the table, but Jill hadn't finished her toast and jam, so Amy sat back down and waited, her head resting dejectedly in her hands.

Suddenly Jill spat out the chewed-up toast on her hand and dumped it on her egg plate.

"Jill, don't spit." Mother sternly handed Jill a napkin to wipe her hands and face.

"There was something hard in that toast." Jill pulled the corners of her mouth down to show that if there was anything she didn't like, it was something hard in the toast.

"Mother!" Amy was surprised out of her depression when she saw Jill's gaping, downturned mouth. "Jill's tooth is gone!"

And it was. There was a big space in Jill's mouth right where one of her bottom front teeth had been.

"Good heavens!" Mother laughed when she saw how funny Jill looked. "I'm certainly glad you didn't swallow it."

Jill began stirring with her finger in the discarded toast.

"Here it is," she announced, proudly holding up her tooth. "That's what was hard in my toast. I'm glad I found my tooth so I can put it under my pillow tonight."

While Amy was drying the dishes, Jeannine called on the telephone.

"Sarah Todd," she said all out of breath and excited to be the bearer of good tidings, "has been selling magazines, and she has to finish canvassing the whole town today so she can spend the last week before school starts with some cousins in Cottonwood. And she said we can help her, Amy—me and you. Sarah has made lots of money this way."

"Oh, Jeannine, how wonderful!"

"She said to come by about noon and she will give us each a subscription book and some sample magazines and will show us which streets to sell on."

Amy danced as she hung up the phone. What luck! Amy wished that Berne were home so that she could tell him.

By the time Amy had finished the dishes, straightened up the living room, and admired Jill's mouth with its new hole ten times, it was nearly noon. Amy put on her white dress with the red polka dots and brushed her hair so she would look nice and people would buy lots of magazines from her. She took a cheese sandwich to eat on the way to the Todd's house.

As she walked along, the sun peeked from behind the swirling clouds overhead for a few minutes. It brightened the whole valley. Amy brightened too, for she was imagining all the money she would earn selling magazines. She might make as much as ten or fifteen dollars. Then she and Berne would be able to buy Desert after all.

Soon she walked by the Todd's hedge and through their gate. Jeannine and Sarah were waiting on the lawn. Sarah quickly showed Amy the subscription book and some folders with pictures in them which described all the exciting things the magazines contained. She gave Amy four sample magazines: the *Gunsman*, a sports magazine; the *Ladies Book*, a magazine about home and food; *Weekly*, a news magazine; and the *Mailbox Magazine*, a magazine for everybody. Sarah explained that she was going to the streets east of town,

Jeannine to the north, and that left the south for Amy.

"I understand," said Amy when she left the Todd's yard.

Amy would rather have had a different section, for she knew none of the people who lived to the south of town, where the homes were small, old, and far apart. And Amy didn't care to sell magazines in the Indian village, which was on the very edge of town, for she only knew two Indians, Eddie Quitchapoo and Marie Chegup, who were in her class at school. They were both very quiet.

Last year Amy was making up the birthday calendar for the class, and when she asked Eddie when his birthday was, he just shrugged as though he didn't know or care. He wouldn't tell her how to spell Quitchapoo either. Amy suspected it was because he didn't know. She had tried to talk to Marie Chegup a few times too, because she was always by herself and didn't have any friends, but Marie looked scared, stared at the ground, and mumbled so softly that Amy couldn't hear her. Once Jeannine told Amy that after school the Indian boys would go out behind the building, heat silver dollars red hot, then hold them on their arms as long as they could to see who was toughest. Amy decided she would go to the Indian houses last.

Amy walked one block past the school and turned onto the street where she was to start. As she looked down the road, she almost lost her courage for just a moment, for the paths that led along the sides of the street were choked with weeds, and lying in the middle of the road was a huge Great Dane. Amy had seen the dog several times in the schoolyard. But it didn't seem to belong to anyone there, for none of the boys teased it. They all stayed out of its way.

Amy told herself that for Desert she would brave anything. But she wished Berne were with her. Luckily she didn't have to pass the dog to get through the gate of the first house, and maybe he would go away before she came out. As she entered the fenced-in yard, she felt encouraged, for the lawn was smooth and green and was banked on every side by many varieties of flowers. She walked onto the gigantic front porch of the ancient two-story brick house and knocked timidly. Almost immediately she heard heavy footsteps behind the door, and it swung open.

"Hello," said a lady who was so fat that she blocked the whole doorway. "Come in, come in."

When she stepped back from the door, Amy went in. The lady's voice was rather gruff and low, but she smiled at Amy and asked her to sit down. She herself plopped down in a big soft chair, stretching her legs way out in front of her.

"My, you're a fine looking girl—yes, you are," the lady began the conversation. "How old are you?" Then without waiting for Amy to answer, she continued, "Do you like chrysanthemums? I just put some in a vase over there. And look, here are some pink petunias. . . ." and the fat lady went on and on about flowers.

Amy unfolded the advertisements and laid the magazines on the arm of her chair. When the fat lady finally stopped for breath, Amy put the picture folder in front of her and began, "I have four kinds of magazines . . ."

But the fat lady, getting her breath again, said, "Yes, dear. My rose bushes haven't done as well this year as last, but I think it's because of the earwigs," and she began talking about earwigs and other bugs that came to eat her flowers.

Amy flipped open the *Ladies Book* to a page with a garden picture. "Here are some pretty flowers," she commented.

"How nice," said the fat lady, and she went on about *how* she planted her flowers and *when* she planted them and *why* she planted just the ones she planted. Then she heaved herself out of her soft chair. "You must see my flowers out in the back."

Amy quickly gathered her magazines and papers together and followed the lady through the house and out the door. The back yard, which was very large, had no lawn, but was completely filled with flowers. The lady led her through the garden telling her about each variety, then around to the front of the house, commenting on every flower on the way. After a long time they reached the gate, and Amy opened it and slipped through.

"You must come again when the rest of the chrysanthemums are blooming," the lady invited. "My, you are a smart girl for your age!"

As Amy walked down the street, the lady bent over and began flipping ants off some roses.

The Great Dane lifted its head and looked toward Amy as she passed a vacant lot which separated the fat lady's yard from the next house, an old two-story brick structure with weeds near it and around the edges of the dry lawn. As she turned in the path that led to the door, Amy carefully watched the dog, which was closely watching her. The moment she stepped onto the porch, the Great Dane leaped to its feet, stood at attention for a moment, then bounded up the street toward her. The dog was so huge and bounded so fast that it reached the porch in a matter of seconds.

But Amy was fast too. She knocked on the door very hard, then crowded between it and the screen. She held her magazines above her head and took a deep breath so that she could pull the screen door tightly shut. The huge dog came very near, staring at her with its saggy, bloodshot eyes and with its long tongue hanging from its mouth. Amy, still holding her breath, pulled harder on the screen door. Just then the wooden door behind her opened. Amy and her magazines crashed backwards to land in a heap on the floor.

"Well, well," said a very skinny old man, bending over her. "Well, well, well."

"Hello," greeted Amy, gathering her papers together, "I'm selling four kinds of magazines."

"Well, well, well," repeated the old man.

Amy stood up and handed him the *Mailbox Magazine*. "This is a nice one."

The old man held it out—as far away from him as his arm was long. He squinted at it, then turned it upside down and squinted at it once again. "I don't see so well anymore," he said, handing it back.

Just at that moment the Great Dane out on the porch barked a tremendous bark. Amy jumped and turned around to make sure the screen door was still between her and the dog.

"What's the matter, Chester?" asked the old man. "Don't you think Chester is a nice dog?" the old man asked Amy.

"He's pretty big," replied Amy evasively.

The skinny man pushed open the screen door and the dog trotted to him, lifting his head to be petted.

"Well, good-bye." Amy edged carefully by the dog and walked rapidly across the porch and down the path. She was glad the man petted the dog until she was well up the street.

At the next house, a small, brown frame one, no one answered Amy's knock. At the last house on the block, a tiny, wrinkled old lady came to the door. Amy told her she was selling four kinds of magazines and began showing them to her, but the lady mumbled something Amy couldn't hear and closed the door.

Amy felt discouraged as she worked her way through the houses on the next street with no better luck. When she turned into the Indian section, black clouds covered the late afternoon sun, but it was still very hot. It seemed even hotter here in the Indian section where there were few lawns or trees and where the dust rose in wisps from the feet of the barefoot children who played in the road. Amy looked for Eddie

Quitchapoo and Marie Chegup but saw nothing of them.

It took Amy over an hour to cover the entire Indian section, and when she was finished, she still hadn't sold a magazine—not one. Most of the Indians said they didn't want any; several of them just peeked out the window without even opening the door; and a few shrugged at her carelessly and said words she didn't understand.

It was early evening when Amy started home, tired and very discouraged. As she walked by the small, brown, frame house which she had passed earlier, she noticed that the front door was open and a radio was playing inside. Certainly someone was home now. Amy decided to try just once more, hoping that she could sell at least one magazine. She walked up the path and knocked. A tall, thin lady opened the screen door.

"Hello," said Amy, "I'm selling magazines."

"Who is it, Esther?" In the kitchen doorway appeared another lady who had a bunch of dripping wet carrots in her hand.

"It's just a little girl selling magazines," replied the lady called Esther.

"Oh, let me see," exclaimed the other lady, dripping water from the carrots all the way over to Amy.

"Well, go ahead and look if you want to, Mabel, but I know there isn't anything I would want." Esther sat down on a saggy couch.

"This is the *Mailbox Magazine*," said Amy wearily.

"*Mailbox Magazine!*" Mabel took the magazine from Amy's hand, sat down in a very worn easy chair and began flipping the pages. "This story called 'Three's a Crowd' looks good."

She broke one carrot off from the bunch and began chewing noisily on it, water dripping slowly from the end of it onto the magazine. She read down the page, making little grunts and giggles above the crunching noise. Amy stood first on one foot, then the other as she waited while Mabel read. Finally Mabel finished the story—and three carrots.

"Oh, Esther," she said, "you've just got to read this."

She handed Esther the open magazine and took the *Ladies Book* from Amy's arms. She broke off another carrot. Esther turned on an old lamp that stood near her, for the room was growing dark.

Amy sat down on a small wooden rocking chair that stood near the door and waited quietly while Esther read "Three's a Crowd," and Mabel read "The Ladies' Man." Then they traded magazines, and Esther read "The Ladies' Man" while Mabel read "The Day Buster was Right." After they traded again, Esther read, "The Day Buster was Right" while Mabel copied some recipes out of the *Ladies Book*.

Amy felt sure they would buy a magazine because they liked them so much. She tried to be patient while she waited, for she hoped it would mean money for Desert. Esther and Mabel traded again, and Amy lost track of which stories they were reading. It was dark outside now and had been for a long time. After they traded several more times, Mabel took the remaining two sample magazines from Amy, and finally gave all the magazines back to Amy.

"Here little girl," she said, and she walked into the kitchen to get another bunch of carrots.

"Goodnight, little girl." Esther held the screen door open for Amy to leave.

Amy's mouth dropped open. "Aren't you going to buy one?" She couldn't believe that they would keep her there all these hours without buying anything.

"They aren't very good magazines," Esther commented, still holding the screen door open. Moths flew in the open door and Esther swatted at them with one hand.

There was nothing more for Amy to say. She walked onto the porch and out into the night. When the door shut behind her, she realized just how dark it was. The storm that had been threatening all day still threatened. Clouds hung low over the valley, blotting out the stars and the moon, and a gusty wind whipped Amy's skirt tight against her legs. She had never been out alone on a night as dark as this. Her feet felt along the weed-choked street, for the darkness around her was much too black to see through.

But as black as the night was, it was not nearly so black as the discouragement in her heart. Amy had not earned one penny all day. Tomorrow they would have to tell Mr. Peneck that they couldn't buy Desert—that he would have to find another buyer. Tears started from Amy's eyes as she thought of someone else buying Desert, someone who would probably call him Duncan.

Amy was so intent in her sorrow that she paid no attention to where she was going. Suddenly the sound of a panting breath right behind her made her stop, frozen in her tracks. With a start, she realized that she must be near the house where the Great Dane lived. Although it was much too dark to see, she was convinced that droopy, bloodshot eyes peered wickedly at her through the night.

With a leap, she started running through the weeds. Once she stepped in a hole and fell sideways, skinning her elbow, and once she ran too close to the fence, tearing her dress on some thorny bushes that grew there. When she reached the end of the block, she slipped on some loose gravel and skidded on her knees out into the street.

For a moment she just lay there, expecting the Great Dane to leap on top of her. Even when nothing happened, she was afraid to move. Her skinned knees began to ache. She was too frightened, hurt, and discouraged to do anything except put her face down in the gravel and cry.

While she lay there in the dark road sobbing, the rain began to fall—rather softly at first, then a little more heavily. Slowly Amy got to her feet. Still sobbing, she walked down the middle of the dark street, the rain drops mixing with her tears as they ran down her face.

She passed the school and the church and turned down her own street. By the time she reached the Thick's yard, most of the tears had stopped, but the rain dripping from her bangs still made little paths down her cheeks. She sloshed through the gutter, into her yard, and onto the porch. Shifting the sopping magazines to her left arm, she pulled the door open and stepped inside. She stood near the door, rain water dripping from her clothes and hair, and colored water streaming from the magazines.

Berne, who was standing near the kitchen door, stared at her unblinkingly, then said nonchalantly,

"Here she is. Here's Amy." Almost immediately Mother, Dad, and the animal doctor popped into the living room.

"Amy Jackson," Mother scolded, but she looked very relieved, "Amy Jackson, where have you been? We've been calling all over for you."

"Amy, Oh, Amy!" Dad moaned sadly as he stared at her. "Amy, oh, Amy."

Amy couldn't hold the tears back when Dad spoke that way. She put the back of her hand over her eyes and began to cry again.

Then everyone seemed to be around her. Berne took the wet magazines from her hands. Dad pulled off her wet shoes, and the animal doctor wiped the tears from her cheeks with his handkerchief. Mother with a big towel rubbed her hair, saying all the time, "Amy dear, Amy dear."

Finally Mother led Amy into the bathroom, took off her wet clothes, washed the gravel out of her skinned knees, and helped her into her pajamas. She tucked her into bed, still saying, "Amy dear, Amy dear," and brought her a bowl of soup and a glass of milk. Although she really wasn't hungry, Amy ate a little, and the food did make her feel better. Soon Mother took the dishes away and switched off the light. Amy lay in bed, her wet hair dampening the pillow. She stayed awake for awhile listening to the soft sound of the rain as it fell outside and feeling very glad to be home.

Chapter 10

It was dismal. When Amy awoke the next morning, the sunshine neither poured into her room nor from her heart. While she dressed, she stood at the window and watched the black clouds that swam around the mountains to the east. August thirty-first, Amy thought, and wished September first wouldn't come at all. For tomorrow Mr. Peneck was leaving Jacksonville, and if they didn't have the money, he would have to sell Desert to someone else.

As Amy took some clean jeans from her drawer, she tried to work up a little hope about the money box and what wasn't in it. But the black clouds were too thick both in the sky and in her heart. Her skinned knees ached as she bent to step into her jeans and her tangled hair flopped sorrowfully down over her eyes as a result of last night's soaking.

Somehow though, the new day even with its dark clouds, seemed to carry promises. As Amy straightened up and pushed the hair from her eyes, her courage came back and she began to believe that some way they would still be able to buy Desert. It may have been the sun, which soon popped through the clouds, or it may have been the animal doctor's funny story about sharing the same shelter with a skunk during yesterday's thunderstorm. But whatever it was, by the time Amy joined Berne on the front lawn a little later, she was humming "And they cut down the old pine tree."

Berne didn't share Amy's enthusiasm for the new day. He sat on the lawn, his chin on his knees, scowling at Vacuum, who was trying to work up some sort of a game with Berne's shoelace. When Amy continued to hum, Berne's scowl grew darker and darker. Although he was looking at Vacuum and not at Amy, she stopped humming and sat silent.

Finally Amy spoke, "This lawn is wet."

"Uh-huh," mumbled Berne.

He wasn't scowling now, but he made no move to get up. Amy didn't move either. She glanced sideways at Berne, but he still didn't look at her. She wondered if he were angry with her, for it had been her idea to give the money to Hurley.

"Hurley really likes his paper route," Amy commented. "Everyone says he's doing a good job."

"Yes," Berne agreed, "it's just what he needed."

He looked straight at Amy and gave her sort of a half smile. Amy was relieved to know that he wasn't angry at her, or at Hurley either, for that matter. They sat on the lawn awhile longer, watching Vacuum as she rubbed up against one of them and then the other.

Berne said very matter-of-factly, "I'd better go over to Mr. Peneck's now and tell him we can't buy Desert. He'll need time today to see if the Williams still want to buy him."

The Williams of Cottonwood, as well as several other people in the valley, had talked to Mr. Peneck about buying Desert. But he had told Berne and Amy that he would rather sell Desert to them than to anyone else.

Amy didn't know why she said next what she did, but she said it with conviction. "Berne, wait until after lunch. Something will turn up. I'm sure it will."

"Oh, Amy," said Berne, scowling again, "what could possibly turn up? Isn't that just like a girl!"

He stood up, and Amy was afraid he was going over to see Mr. Peneck right then. She was glad when he walked leisurely to the house and leaned against the porch rail. Amy moved to the steps near him.

Jill came out of the house with two left-over pancakes stuck together with honey. When Vacuum sniffed hungrily at them, she climbed on the porch rail and sat there hanging over in both directions.

"Let's go to Mr. Peneck's," Jill coaxed with her mouth full.

Amy groaned inwardly. Trust Jill to say the wrong thing!

"Yes, I guess I'd better go," Berne decided, "but *you* can't go, Jill."

"I want to go to Mr. Peneck's. Let me come too. Please, please, please, please, please."

Amy was afraid Berne would walk out of the yard on his way to Mr. Peneck's at that very moment just to show Jill that she couldn't go.

Berne frowned long at Jill, but he remained leaning on the porch rail. While Berne was still looking crossly at Jill, Dad stepped out of the house onto the front porch.

"I guess tomorrow is your big day," he smiled.

Neither Berne nor Amy spoke.

"Well, how much do I owe you?" he continued, taking out his wallet.

"With the money that I earned yesterday, just thirty-four dollars and sixteen cents," Berne replied.

Dad stared first at Berne and then at Amy. "But I thought you had your fifty dollars earned weeks ago."

"We did," Berne stared hard at the ground, "but we haven't got it now."

"How do you expect to buy a horse if you can't save and plan for it?" asked Dad, putting his wallet back in his pocket. He didn't sound very pleased with them.

"We don't," Berne answered. "I was just going over to Mr. Peneck's to tell him we can't buy Desert."

Dad looked angry. "Well, it isn't right to wait

until the last minute to tell Mr. Peneck. You'd better high-tail it over to see him right now." He turned to go in the house.

Amy hadn't thought Dad would be angry with them. Now Berne was scowling again.

"It wasn't Berne's fault." Amy jumped up and followed her father to the screen door. "I was the one who thought of it."

"Thought of what?" asked Dad.

"Of giving our money away," Amy answered.

"Of giving it away?"

"Yes, that's why we haven't got the fifty dollars."

"But it was all right with me," confessed Berne, "and I gave it to him."

"What *are* you children talking about?" asked Dad. "Who did you give the money to?"

"To Hurley," said Amy, "for his paper route."

"She means for his bicycle," Berne corrected. "He couldn't have the paper route without a bike, so we gave him twenty-five dollars."

Dad took off his cowboy hat and tapped it gently on his knee for a moment. The angry creases slowly disappeared from around his eyes.

"I see." He let go of the screen-door handle. "Then you've earned quite a bit more than fifty dollars. I said I would give you as much money as you earned. How much have you earned all together?"

"Oh, how much have we, Berne?" Amy asked.

It took Berne a moment to do the necessary arithmetic. "Fifty-nine dollars and sixteen cents."

Dad pulled out his wallet again. "Well, I guess that's how much I owe you," he said. He counted out fifty-eight dollars, but had to go in the house and get one dollar and sixteen cents in change from Mother. He handed the money to Berne, then turned and stepped inside the screen door.

Amy flew to Berne's room and returned with the box labeled DESERT.

"I knew something would turn up," she beamed. "Now we can buy Desert."

"We still haven't quite enough," said Berne practically. He put the money Dad had given him in the box, then wrote on a paper:

Earned	$34.16
From Dad	59.16
Total	$93.32

"We still need six dollars and sixty-eight cents. How can we earn six dollars and sixty-eight cents in just one day?"

"You could go rabbit hunting," suggested Amy, "and I'll call Sheriff Jensen to see if he wants beans picked from his garden and Mrs. Anchor to see if she needs help with the children."

"It wouldn't be enough." Berne shook his head. "We've got to think of something else."

He looked far away as if he were thinking of something else. Amy tried to think of something else too, but if there was another way to earn money, she had no idea what it could be.

"I know," Berne snapped his fingers. "We'll sell something."

Usually Amy thought Berne had good ideas—very good ideas. But this didn't sound like one to her. She had tried selling things—magazines and jewelry—and she couldn't see how they could possibly earn six dollars and sixty-eight cents selling anything in one day.

"Well, I guess we could try," said Amy hesitantly, "but I don't know."

Jill, who had been listening, jumped down from the porch rail and ran over to them. "I'll be the display."

"What display?" asked Berne.

"We let her be the model when we sold bead jewelry," Amy explained.

"We aren't going to sell jewelry or any silly trinkets," Berne scoffed. "We'll have to sell something valuable."

"Valuable?" asked Amy. "Like what?"

"Like your big doll or my pump gun," said Berne. "Don't you know someone who would want to buy something like that?"

Amy rubbed her forehead thoughtfully. She knew that Jeannine didn't have six dollars and sixty-eight cents with which to buy Amy's big doll. Sarah Todd was too old for big dolls; she liked little ones. Jill would like to buy it, but she only had a few dimes and nickels in her bank. Berne still looked thoughtful, so Amy kept trying to think of someone who would buy her big doll.

At that moment Hurley came zooming down the road on his new bike. He made a half circle and skidded to a stop on the gravel of the roadside in front of the Jacksons' yard. He swung his leg over the bar and kicked the stand down just as Winston, all out of breath, ran up to join him. They walked into the Jacksons' yard and up to the porch where Berne and Amy were sitting.

"Hi, Hurley," greeted Berne.

"Hi, Berne," Hurley replied. He stood in front of them, jerking at his worn shirt collar. But he didn't say anything else.

"Hi, Hurley," Amy finally added encouragingly.

"Hi, Amy," Hurley growled, tugging so hard at his collar that Amy was afraid it would tear.

Winston moved over by Jill, who was licking honey off her hands. "What ya doing?" he asked.

"Eating honey. Do you want some?" She held out one hand for Winston to sample.

Winston licked the finger nearest him. "It doesn't taste like honey to me; it tastes like hand."

"You didn't taste the right place." Jill pointed to a sticky spot, but Winston didn't want to try again, so Jill finished it herself.

"Hi, Berne and Amy," Hurley repeated still pulling nervously at his shirt. Finally he shoved his right hand deep into his pocket and pulled out some money. "Here," he said gruffly. He thrust the money into Berne's hand.

"What's this for?" asked Berne, looking first at

Hurley and then at the money. There were some dollar
bills and a little change.

"It's part of the money I owe you," Hurley answered, scuffing his shoe against the porch.

"But you don't have to pay us back," said Berne.
"We gave you the money."

"I know," said Hurley, "but I want to. I wish I
could pay it all back right now so you could use it for
Desert." When Hurley said this he kicked his toe so
hard against the bottom step that he hopped on one
foot for a moment afterwards.

"But where did you ever get it?" asked Amy, looking at Hurley with wonder.

"I sold my catcher's mitt to Billy Jensen. He gave me six dollars and twenty-five cents for it."

Berne opened his hand and counted the money silently. "Six dollars and twenty-five cents," he said.

"Oh, Hurley," cried Amy, "your nice catcher's mitt!" Amy remembered how proud Hurley had been of his mitt last spring. His grandmother had sent it to him. He brought it to school and showed everyone until the entire class was tired of hearing him say in his gruff voice that with that mitt he could catch any ball, no matter how fast.

"I can buy another one," Hurley shrugged, "now that I have the paper route. Come on, Winston." He strode toward his bike with Winston following at his heels.

"That's sure swell of you," Berne called to Hurley as he swung on his bike and began pumping away. Hurley raised his hand to wave at them as he rode out of sight with Winston running along behind.

"It must have been pretty hard to sell his nice catcher's mitt," commented Amy.

"Yes," said Berne, "pretty swell of him." He put the six dollars and twenty-five cents in the box and added on the paper:

$$\begin{array}{lr} \text{Total} & \$93.32 \\ \text{From Hurley} & 6.25 \\ \hline & \$99.57 \end{array}$$

"We just need forty-three cents, and that should be easy to get." Berne stood up. "I'll get my pump gun and go rabbit hunting."

Jill, who was hanging over the porch rail by her knees, her head dangling into the irises, asked, "If I helped buy Desert, would he be part mine?"

"I guess so," said Berne generously.

"Wait right here," she ordered.

She hopped down from the porch rail and scampered into the house. In a minute she was back holding out her bank. "I've really got a lot of money now. Tooths are worth a lot of money." She pulled down her lip again to show them the hole.

Berne opened the bank and counted out forty-three cents.

"There, that's your change." He handed Jill the bank which still held nine cents.

Jill tucked the bank under her arm, jumped on the porch rail and pretended she was riding Desert.

Berne dropped the forty-three cents in the money box. "Well, there it is," he said, shaking the box gently with both hands. He smiled at Amy.

"I knew something would turn up," Amy grinned back at him.

"And it did. It sure did." Berne began whistling, "I'm an Old Cowhand from the Rio Grande."

Chapter 11

The morning of September first dawned bright and clear. When Amy went down to the kitchen, Mother was busy making a cake, but she stopped long enough to hand Amy a plate of scrambled eggs. Jill, who had finished her breakfast for the second time, was wiping out her cereal bowl with a piece of bread. Amy looked at the eggs, but her stomach felt funny—like it had the night they first asked Dad if they could buy Desert.

"Jill," she asked, "would you like some of my scrambled eggs?"

"Yes." Jill speared a big section of eggs with a fork and put it on some toast. Amy watched her eat the sandwich, but she couldn't bring herself to as much as nibble the eggs left on her plate.

Jill finished the egg and toast, then looked long-ingly at the rest of Amy's eggs. "Want me to eat some more?" she asked.

"Yes," said Amy, pushing the plate in front of Jill, who gobbled them up, then ran into the bathroom to brush her teeth. Amy put the empty plate in the sink and followed Jill into the bathroom.

As Amy reached for her toothbrush, she noticed Jill standing in front of the sink, rubbing her teeth thoughtfully with her finger.

"Know what?" Jill asked, "the up teeth go down and the down teeth go up."

Amy wondered how Jill could waste so much time on such a special morning. "Hurry and brush your teeth. Desert will be here soon."

Jill was indignant. "I *am* brushing my teeth!"

"With your finger?" asked Amy.

Jill pulled her finger out of her mouth to show Amy the toothpaste on it. "I can't find my toothbrush," she said in way of explanation. "I think I left it outside yesterday."

Amy finished brushing her teeth and left the bath-room, where Jill was still standing in front of the sink rubbing her teeth and philosophizing.

When Amy stepped out the back door, Berne waved to her from the yard.

"Amy, come and see," he called.

As she followed him to the barn, Amy shivered a little although she certainly wasn't cold.

"Dad says we can keep him in here." Berne swung

open the huge wooden door to a large room, the upper half of which opened directly onto the hayloft. "I've been cleaning it."

"Oh, it looks nice," Amy marveled. "It really does."

Berne had swept it out and put hay in the manger. He really wouldn't have needed the hay, for there was still plenty of pasture this time of year.

"Dad says Desert can use the big corral that opens off this part of the barn, and while the weather is good, we can leave the corral gate open so he can go down the lane to the pasture on Clear Creek."

"Oh, Berne, it's just perfect!" sighed Amy. That funny feeling in her stomach caused her to draw her breath in quickly. She began to laugh and dance around the barn that soon would be Desert's home.

At that moment the barn door opened and in popped Jill. "Is Desert here yet?" she asked. Winston, who had been following her, peeked around the door frame.

"Not yet," said Berne.

"Oh," Jill giggled, "I'm so de-cited I don't know what to do."

"Climb up into the hayloft," said Berne, "that would be something to do. Then throw me down the halter that's hanging on the nail there."

"I can do it easy," bragged Jill, " 'cause I'm five."

She climbed up the ladder, which was nailed to the wall, and into the hayloft. Winston dashed to the ladder and followed her up. When Jill tossed the halter down, Berne hung it on a nail by the door where it would be handy to put on Desert when Mr. Peneck brought him.

"I did it easy," stated Jill, " 'cause I'm five."

"Ah—" said Winston, "I know a girl who is six and I can beat her up."

"Can you?" asked Jill, very interested.

"Ya," said Winston, "and I can beat you up too, but I won't."

" 'Cause you love me?"

" 'Cause I like you."

Suddenly they heard a commotion in the barn-yard. Berne hurriedly pushed open the big door and dashed out. There by the chicken coop was Mr. Peneck, riding his brown mare, and following closely behind him on a rope was Desert, his light mane bobbing as he swung his head up to look around. His sorrel coat gleamed even through the dust that was stirred up by his proud feet as he stepped through the barnyard.

"Oh, Berne," Amy exclaimed. "Oh, Berne!" That was all she could say, over and over again, for Desert seemed grander to her than ever before. She almost believed for a minute that he *was* the ghost horse that Jill had once thought him.

"He sure is like Great-grandfather's horse," said Berne.

Mr. Peneck swung down from the mare. "Well, do you still want him?" he asked gruffly, but smiling all the while into the children's radiant faces.

"Oh yes, Mr. Peneck, oh yes!" And Amy kept saying "oh yes" the way she had been saying "oh Berne" before.

The next few minutes were ones of confusion, for Jill and Winston ran around and around the horses. Mother, Dad, and the animal doctor came from the house and stood by chattering. Berne took a huge envelope out of his pocket and began counting out the money into Mr. Peneck's hands. Even Hurley walked up the driveway and stood grinning with his hands in his pockets as he watched the excitement. With so many people moving around and the horses pacing nervously, the dust of the barnyard began to rise in billowy clouds around them.

And everyone was talking at once—everyone except Amy. She walked up to Desert and stood very still not saying a word. Desert lowered his head. Amy carefully reached toward him, touched his nose, and slid her hand slowly down it. Desert didn't seem to mind at all, so she stroked the side of his face with the other hand. As she carefully slid her free hand up into his mane, still stroking the side of his face, the horse stopped pawing at the barnyard dust.

"Desert," Amy spoke softly, "Desert, Desert, Desert——"

When Hurley had gone off to ride his bike, and Jill and Winston had gone to play in the hayloft; when Mother, Dad, and the animal doctor had gone back into the house, and Berne had run to the barn to find a curry comb and brush; when Mr. Peneck had ridden off on his mare, and the dust had cleared, Amy was still standing with one hand in Desert's mane and the other hand stroking his face, saying "Desert, Desert, Desert, Desert."

Dad began to break Desert that very day. Desert was smart and soon became an excellent saddle horse. The animal doctor was able to ride him before he left Jacksonville in the middle of September, and it wasn't too many weeks before Desert was broken so well that Mother didn't object to the children riding him.

To Mother, Desert became a safe horse. To Dad, Desert became a well-trained horse. To Jill, Desert became a fun horse. To Berne, Desert became the smartest horse in Jacksonville and even all Cottonwood. To all of them he was a fine horse. But to Amy he was something more. When she would go into the barn and put one hand in his mane and stroke his face with the other, she knew that he was good—the way Great-grandfather's Desert had been good. And she felt good too—like Great-grandfather was good.

When she would ride him over the rough clods of the lane or through the tall weeds of the roadside, she knew that Desert was brave—the way Great-grandfather's Desert was brave. And she felt brave too—like Great-grandfather was brave.

So that's how Amy felt about Desert, and it was how Desert felt about Amy too.

It was one day after she had been in the barn petting him that Amy discovered the secret of the wondrous deeds of Great-grandfather's horse. She came in the house to help Mother set the table for dinner.

"Mother," she sighed, "I do love that horse."

"He loves you too," Mother replied.

"He's good and brave, and he's wondrous. He could do anything in the world, even—even—swim the Yampa River or give warning against rattlesnakes or find lost children—or—anything. I'm sure he could," Amy said certainly.

"I'm sure he could too," said Mother. "For you. I'm sure he could for you."

About the Author

Laura Fisher grew up on a farm in southeastern Idaho. The fourth child in a family of eight, Mrs. Fisher describes herself then as an "in-betweener . . . too young to be wanted in the games of the older children and too old to enjoy playing with the younger ones." Despite this plight, however, Mrs. Fisher's childhood ran the gamut of experience from the time when, as a three-year-old she received a Sunday School award for her quiet demeanor in class until in high school she was honored with the Babe Ruth Sportsmanship Award for being a rambunctious sportswoman!

When she was not being chased with spiders or snakes by older brothers and sisters, or falling off "the usual number of horses," Mrs. Fisher spent her happiest childhood hours by a creek (much like Amy's Clear Creek) that ran through the pasture of the farm.

Mrs. Fisher's writing career began in high school when she served as assistant editor of the school newspaper. Her interest in children's books developed when her own children reached reading age. In her search for books for them she "discovered an area of writing about which I knew nothing . . . I was surprised, elated, and inspired." Out of this discovery and enthusiasm her first story for children has evolved.

Mrs. Fisher received her BA degree from Brigham Young University. She and her husband and their three young children now reside in Wyoming, where Mr. Fisher is a professor at the state university.